Books in the Dragonflight Series

The Wizard's APPRENTICE

by S. P. Somtow

Illustrated by
NICHOLAS
JAINSCHIGG

A Byron Preiss Book

Atheneum   1993   New York

Maxwell Macmillan Canada
Toronto

Maxwell Macmillan International
New York   Oxford   Singapore   Sydney

THE WIZARD'S APPENTICE
Dragonflight Books

Cover painting by Nicholas Jainschigg. Cover and interior design by Dean Motter.
Edited by John Betancourt.

Special thanks to Jonathan Lanman, Leigh Grossman, and Howard Kaplan

Atheneum
Macmillan Publishing Company
866 Third Avenue
New York, NY 10022

Maxwell Macmillan Canada, Inc.
1200 Eglinton Avenue East
Suite 200
Don Mills, Ontario M3C 3N1

Macmillan Publishing Company is part of the Maxwell Communication Group of
Companies.

First edition
Printed in the United States of America
10 9 8 7 6 5 4 3 2 1

Somtow, S. P.
    The wizard's apprentice / by S.P. Somtow; illustrated by Nicholas Jainschigg. —
1st ed.
        p.   cm. —(Dragonflight series)
    "A Byron Preiss book."
    Summary: A wizard recruits a rich teenager from Los Angeles to be his next
apprentice.
    ISBN 0–689–31576–7
    [1. Magic—Fiction. 2. Wizards—Fiction. 3. Los Angeles (Calif.)—
Fiction.] I. Jainschigg, Nicholas, ill. II. Title. III. Series.
PZ7.S69735Wi   1993
[Fic]—dc20   93–12384

For Conan Yuzna:
Have a great birthday!

Contents

1

A Magic Kingdom

In the city of Los Angeles, on the northern slopes of the Santa Monica Mountains, there lies a magic kingdom called Encino. It is a land of glittering shopping malls, Japanese bank buildings, sushi bars, and German cars; of video arcades, fast-food havens, and casually dressed people with wallets full of credit cards; of neon, palm trees, and smog.

Encino is often, by the casual tourist, mistaken for paradise; only those who live there know that all is not glitz and glitter. There *is* magic in Encino all right, but it is not in the shopping malls, sushi bars, Porsches, and credit cards. It is the kind of magic you can find anywhere, if you have the vision to see it and the courage to grasp hold of it and the strength of heart not to give in to the dark forces that guard it. For, you see, every kingdom is a magic kingdom, and every story, when correctly viewed, is about magic.

1

Except that most people never find out these things.

It is the first day of summer, in the final decade of the twentieth century, and a high school sophomore named Aaron Maguire is about to find out all about magic. He doesn't know it yet, of course, because school is out and magic is the furthest thing from his mind. When he's in a good mood he thinks about hanging out at the Galleria, trying to get Penelope Karpovsky to go out with him, and talking his father into letting him use his May Company charge card. When he's in a bad mood, he thinks mostly about his parents' impending divorce and what he's going to say when the judge finally pops him the question that hangs over his head like a personal thundercloud: *Who do you want to live with, Aaron? Your mom or your dad?*

For the time being, Aaron's parents are separated, but neither of them wants to give up the million-dollar house, halfway up the hill, with its commanding view of the San Fernando Valley and its enormous entertainment potential. Of course, neither of his parents has done any entertaining since they stopped getting along, somewhere around the time Aaron was in the seventh grade.

In the meantime, the house has been split off into two opposing "spheres of influence." The Cold War may be over, but something like it continues, in miniature, at the Maguires' house. There is a line through the middle of the living room, from the northeast tip of the Persian rug to the southwest corner of the Italian credenza. The line may be invisible, but its effects are as palpable as those of the former Berlin Wall.

The western half of the living room—his mother's side— is simply and tastefully adorned. The sofa and loveseat are in southwestern pastels, and a print by Chagall complements the ensemble. Aaron's mother is a buyer for one of the most exclusive boutiques in Beverly Hills, and her half of the house reflects what she does for a living: It's elegant, subtle, and never, never overstated.

Aaron's father's end of the living room, by contrast, is a jungle. On the wall is a frayed poster of the movie *Drenched in Gore,* which is billed as "featuring the gore-drenched effects of Hollywood's 'wizard of splatter,' Beau Maguire." On the floor is a three-headed latex monster built for the movie *The Beast That Threw Up Schenectady.* It's no longer operational, but it's still plugged into the wall, and occasionally, when there's a power surge or a brownout, it can be seen gnashing its teeth or clawing at the air. Against one wall is a battered green sofa with a pile of magazines; the cover of the one on top shows the selfsame beast in all its slimy splendor, with the caption: *Beau Maguire—The Wizard Bats a Thousand.* Next to the sofa, a door leads directly into a workshop that used to be a garage.

Aaron's mother's side of the house includes the back patio, with the jacuzzi; his father's side encompasses the swimming pool. His mother's side contains the library; his father's has the kitchen, which is a shame because his father doesn't know how to cook.

Since Aaron's parents have joint custody, Aaron has two rooms, one on either side of the house. During school, he lives with his mother during the week and with his father on weekends; during the school vacation, it's alternating weeks.

This week, the first week of summer, is one of his father's weeks. His parents' divorce is slowly inching toward a court hearing, and both parents' lawyers are trying to get hold of him. Aaron's not thinking about magic at all today. He just wants to get away. His mother is in Bangkok buying sapphires and his father's on a low-budget movie location somewhere in Tucson, but even though he's alone in the house he feels crowded because all the phones are ringing off the hook.

Maybe it's Penelope on the phone, but it's more likely to be one of the lawyers. He wants to pick up, just in case it *is* Penelope, but the likelihood is kind of small—maybe one chance in a million.

3

Better not to answer at all.

Aaron is pacing up and down the living room. He's cranked up the stereo but it doesn't seem to drown out the phones. They have four lines at the Maguire house—his mother's line, his father's line, a fax machine, and Aaron's own phone, which is shaped like a Porsche.

At last Aaron gets tired of listening to all the phones ringing. He marches from room to room, switching on all the answering machines, even his own. He turns the music up so loud that even he gets a little worried that his mother's Ming spittoon may fall off its shelf. Then again—since his parents are out of town—he could always tell them there's been an earthquake. A *little* one, you know, a four-point-five or so, not enough to make the news but *just* enough to send that blue-and-white seven-hundred-year-old spittoon crashing to the ground.

Aaron sits on the battered couch on the Dad side and rests his feet on a Louis XV ottoman on the Mom side of the living room—something he wouldn't dream of doing if either of his parents were home. The music washes over him and he starts to imagine the scene . . . the pieces of the spittoon all over the Persian rug . . . the car pulls into the driveway . . . "Mom . . . there was like, this earthquake." He's standing there, pointing to the floor, as his mother walks in from the hall, jet-lagged to the gills.

He hears his mother's scream of anguish, so piercingly real that it cuts through two hundred watts of heavy metal. He looks up. My God, he thinks, the spittoon has moved an inch or so closer to the edge of the wall unit, and the glass shelf is vibrating.

Aaron panics and turns off the stereo. The Ming spittoon wobbles to a stop. In the sudden pause, there comes a plaintive voice from the answering machine in his westerly bedroom. . . .

"Aaron . . . you wimp! Listen . . . I heard it from Mitzi,

4

who heard it from Gloria, who heard it from Buffy, who heard it from Brad . . . Is it really true that you're the one who sent me that secret admirer note last week? . . . I mean, cool! Don't you realize that I've been trying to get you to notice me for like a month?"

Penelope! Aaron thinks. He starts to run toward the bedroom. He trips over the beast that threw up Schenectady. He hears the refrigerator hum, realizes that when it draws power it causes an automatic brownout, and disengages himself from the beast before it starts to snap its jaws and lunge. He makes it to the corridor. The bedroom's only two doors down. The door's open and he hears Penelope's voice, closer now. . . .

"I bet you're home and you're just too shy to pick up the phone or something . . . so all I'm going to say is this . . . I'm going to be at the mall . . . I'll be standing outside the Thai-Israeli-Mexican Pizza Paradise in exactly thirty minutes and maybe you'll be there too . . . and maybe not. I hope you don't think I'm like being aggressive or anything, but this has gone on long enough . . . *Someone's* got to do something."

"Penelope!"

She hangs up just as he picks up the phone.

I've gotta get down there right now, he thinks.

Usually Aaron's pretty laid back, but he's not going to let an opportunity like this slip through his fingers. He grabs his skateboard from the closet and races out the front door, pausing only to set the burglar alarm before he dashes out onto Milagro Drive.

From Aaron's house, Milagro starts out steep, giving skaters that extra bit of acceleration, and then proceeds at an almost level grade until just short of Ventura Boulevard, when it dives into an unbanked corkscrew and an abrupt uphill curve around which it is possible to execute any number of precision moves. Even though Aaron's in a hurry, he can't help indulging in a few ollies, half-ollies, reverse, inverse, retrograde and free-form ollies, not to mention a few moves so

5

complex that they have no names. Not that Aaron's a champion or anything, but something happens to him when he leaps onto that skateboard. He is instantly transformed from a klutz into a kind of work of art. Rather like a Mozart allegro—lean and lyrical and lightning-fast.

You might almost call this transformation magic.

Today, though, the sonata is cut off in midphrase. Aaron swoops down, hits the dip of the uphill curve, soars up in a tornadoing twist, and bumps smack into someone who wasn't there only a second ago.

Me.

Anaxagoras. Wizard and recruiter of wizards. Ten thousand years old and fit as a fiddle. He doesn't know it, of course, but our meeting has been written in the book of fate since the beginning of time. Aaron looks up at me. He wonders why he can't just walk past me. After all, a blue Acura Legend just went careening past. But he can't squeeze by. It feels as though I've thrown a wall of Saran Wrap across Milagro Drive. It's not cellophane at all, of course. What I've done is cocooned him in a bubble of slowed-down time.

"Greetings, O Aaron," I say softly. "I've been waiting for this moment for a long, long time." This is a corny thing to say, but it's the kind of thing they expect, after reading too many high-fantasy trilogies and watching too many low-budget *Conan* rip-offs.

"Let go of me," Aaron says. "I'm totally in a hurry. Hey, here's a dollar. I mean, I know times are tough for you guys."

He hands me a crinkled bank note. He looks up at me, a tousle-haired blond boy with a winning smile and just a hint of acne; his eyes tell me that he has compassion. This is good. It is one of the requirements.

"Oh, Aaron, Aaron," I tell him, "I'm not one of the homeless. I am a powerful wizard. I have come from the dark dimension to seek out one who possesses the gift of wizardry, that I may train him to become as powerful as myself one day, and to take his place among the great wizards of the transdimensional wizard council when my time has come and gone."

He starts to laugh. "Look, mister," he says—he's looking for a polite way to brush me off, but bless him, he doesn't want to hurt my feelings—"you hear a lot of strange stuff in this town, and I've met some people with some pretty weird job descriptions, but a talent scout for major league wizardry—I mean, give me a break! The girl of my dreams is waiting for me at the mall and I'm gonna miss out if I don't make it down there in fifteen minutes. Just take the dollar, dude, I mean it."

"You'd better take another look at that dollar," I tell him, and he does, and he does one of those cartoon-type double takes, because I've spirited the dollar bill across the dimensional wasteland and replaced it with a freshly minted C-note plucked from the Treasury in Washington.

"How'd you do that?" he says.

"Smoke and mirrors. Mostly mirrors, in this case. Just a dab of smoke. Otherwise people don't think it's real."

"I—" He starts coughing. I could have sworn I got rid of the smoke. Perhaps it's only the smog. The air quality index is worse than usual today.

"Go ahead. Keep it. Plenty more where that came from. And now that I've got your attention . . ."

But I think I'll let Aaron speak for himself now. After all, this is his story, not mine. A good wizard is seen and not heard . . . and a *great* wizard is neither seen nor heard. The best wizards do their work and vanish without a trace. Only the most observant of normal humans can detect the light flash of a magical mirror.

Or a telltale puff of smoke.

2

The Vision Thing

So there I was, fifteen minutes away from the most important meeting of my life, and a homeless dude was standing there telling me hey, I'm a wizard, a wizard talent scout, and you, kid, are the talent I'm scouting. I stood there with my skateboard under my arm holding a hundred-dollar bill that hadn't been there before, and I stared into the old man's eyes.

He *was* old, wasn't he? But he was already changing before my eyes. The tattered Hawaiian shirt was transforming into a cloak with stars and moons on it, and the stars *moved;* they whirled across dark emptiness. And his beard was longer, too. And whiter. The oddest thing was, a couple of people walked uphill, right past us, and they didn't seem to notice him at all.

"Five minutes," I said. "But after that I really have to

go. You have no idea how much this means to me." I looked at my watch. Maybe Penelope's would be running slow.

"Five minutes, one hundred dollars," said the wizard. "You drive a hard bargain."

"C'mon, please." I looked past him, wondering if there was a hidden camcorder in the oleander bushes. That's what it had to be, some kind of candid camera deal. My friends would see it on late-night MTV and make fun of me, especially since I'd forgotten to comb my hair. Hey, but it wouldn't be all bad. It was still free publicity.

Unless it was actually magic.

Well, I thought, maybe I'd better play along. "What makes you think I'm the one you're looking for?" I asked him. "I mean like, I even have trouble pulling rabbits out of hats and making coins disappear. I don't think I'd have much luck, you know, fighting dragons or whatever it is you dudes are supposed to do for a living."

"You're wrong there, Aaron. You have a lot of talent. How do you think you were able to manage that last retrograde ollie?"

"Just practice," I said uneasily.

Well, Anaxagoras the Wizard whips out this solar calculator and does some rapid-fire finger picking of his own, and then he's all, "That, Aaron, is where you're wrong," and shoves the calculator in front of my nose.

This calculator: It had kind of an LCD screen, and on it was a video image of myself hurtling down Milagro Drive and hurling myself into the dip and boomeranging back up. There were mathematical figures dancing on the screen, and finally there was a tabular readout. This is what it said:

SUBJECT: Aaron Maguire

AGE: 16

INTELLIGENCE: Average to Bright

MANEUVER EXECUTED: Retrograde Ollie:
Alsatian Variation

LAWS OF SCIENCE BROKEN: 3 (Three)*

    a. Law of Conservation of Momentum

    b. Third Law of Motion

    c. Law of Gravity

*Newtonian physics used as basis for calculation

**PROBABILITY OF UNCONSCIOUS MAGICAL
FORCES:** 93.7%

"So you see," said the wizard, "I didn't say it; the computer said it. That makes it a fact."

I'm all, "Unconscious magical forces? What are you talking about? You mean I was using magic, and I didn't even know it?"

"It's very scientific," he said. "Some people have an intuitive ability to tap into the unseen dimensions and to draw out streams of energy. This energy can be used for . . . oh, tremendous things. Building rainbow bridges in the sky. Soaring through the night on wings of insubstantial air. And little things, like those deft little skating maneuvers none of your friends can ever quite imitate."

"But I'm not good at skating," I said. "My two friends Andy and Randy—now, *they're* amazing skaters. They've had their pictures in *Thrasher* magazine and they've been in two skateboard videos. Me, I can do a few tricks, but I can never do them twice the same."

"Precisely! You are *not* good at skating, my boy, but you *are* good at magic! Tell me, for example . . . how did you

11

manage to shut off the stereo in the actual fraction of a second that Penelope called you?"

"It was because of the Ming spittoon and . . . wait a minute! . . . How did you know about that?"

"And why did the Ming spittoon wobble its way to the very edge of the shelf just in time so you'd notice and not miss that phone message?"

"I—" This was beginning to sound dangerously convincing.

"A series of amazing coincidences such as would merit a ten-page monograph of the *Journal of Irreproducible Results,*" said Anaxagoras. "And these things have happened before. Just when you think the world is about to end, you're pulled out of the frying pan by an uncanny bout of luck."

It was true. There'd been the time I was supposed to keep Dad out of the house because of a surprise party the people at the studio were throwing, and he insisted on running back into the house because he hadn't added enough brown sugar to the blood. I mean the special effects blood, which is made of corn syrup and food coloring. The brown sugar thickens it to the right texture so it'll photograph right. Anyway, he had to have three gallons of thickness B ready by the midnight shoot and he was having a spaz about it. And he turned right around at the corner and drove back to the house, but *just* as he got to the door (I was going to sprint over to the back patio to warn the party setter-uppers) an enormous bird flew by and doodooed on his head, delaying him long enough for me to give the requisite warning.

I wondered whether that was the kind of anecdote that went over big in the *Journal of Irreproducible Results.*

"Look, kid," the wizard said, and this time he was quite serious. It seemed to me that the whole of Milagro Drive was shrouded in mist. The mist was tendriling around fire hydrants, siphoning from the oleanders, wisping around the trunks of the palm trees. His eyes were glowing an eerie neon green. His voice was deeper, metallic, resonant.

Okay, none of this was that unusual for the son of a special effects wizard. The fog? A/B fog, my dad calls it. It's made by spraying two chemicals into the air at the same time. There's a chemical reaction that causes the fog to condense instantly—a very cheap effect, particularly common in low-budget films where it is necessary to hide the floor. A layer of mist is all the difference between an alien landscape and a sleazy downtown warehouse. The voice? Adjusting the EQ. The glowing eyes? Contact lenses—or atropine eyedrops plus an ultraviolet lamp.

I'd seen it all before. None of it fazed me. But I'm just as much a sucker for movie magic as any yokel from the boonies, and what the wizard had to say was compelling. I found myself just staring at him. Believing.

"Kid," he said, "you're a find in a million. You're the child of nature with the ability to see the Holy Grail where others see only emptiness." Child of nature? I thought. I tried roughing it in Yosemite once. Talked my dad into getting a motel room the next day. It turned out he hated the lack of air conditioning as much as I did; just thought it was the manly thing to do, you know, take your son out into the wilderness, male bonding, get in touch with the inner child, and all that. "Give me a few hours of your time. You'll still get back to the mall in time to see Penelope Karpovsky, I promise, for time is an elastic waistband on the jockey shorts of reality."

"All right." If he could make one dollar into a hundred dollars, he could probably make a couple of hours into fifteen minutes.

"You see, it's not just that you have this innate talent. About one in a thousand has these talents to the extent you have. But to become a wizard takes more than just talent. We look for certain other qualities too. Intelligence, to be sure . . . My computer pegs you at "average to bright," but we've had a number of "genius level" types go berserk and turn to the dark side. But compassion too. You notice that I drew a veil of illusion over myself and you thought I was one of the homeless . . . but instead of walking swiftly past, or looking away, you tried to give me a dollar."

"I don't know if that's really compassion . . . more like liberal guilt . . . It's a big thing here in Encino."

"But also there's another quality that a wizard must have, you see. It's a kind of aloneness. A feeling of being set apart. Orphans are good, but you're not too far from one; I mean, how is it that someone your age is left to fend for himself, with one parent in Bangkok and the other in Tucson? Oh, I know you'll say you're perfectly old enough and your friends' parents do it all the time too, but let's face it: you're pretty mad about it. And about the divorce, and the fact that the lawyers keep calling you and trying to get you to pick sides."

He was right. I was past being surprised that he knew so much about me. I don't think I realized just how mad I was until that moment. I tried to squeeze past the wizard, tried to look away from that piercing gaze; I wanted to scream at him like, how dare you know all these things that even I don't know about me, how dare you ruin the first day of the perfect summer vacation . . . how dare you try to do my parents' job for them.

"So my parents aren't getting along. That hardly makes me any different than most of the kids in the Valley."

"Nevertheless—the talent . . . the vision . . . the compassion . . . the aloneness . . . and the computer readouts . . . You see, it's all very scientific. And, well, I'm offering you a chance to discover the secrets of the universe . . . to believe six impossible things before breakfast . . . even to fight dragons, if that's your thing . . . though once you've seen one, you've seen 'em all."

I guess that that was when I decided to give it a try. If he was telling me the truth, and time was as elastic as that, I could still get over to the mall before Penelope walked out of my life. And if not . . . I thought it over very carefully as I

folded up the hundred-dollar bill and stuck it in my wallet. I'd always been a pretty average kind of guy. Average in school, average in baseball, even, when you compared me to some of my friends, average in skating. I'd always felt that there was *something* I excelled at, if I could only know what it was. The things this dude was saying to me were crazy, but they had a ring of truth. I can't explain how I knew this. Maybe it was my hidden talent at work, this vision thing. And Anaxagoras had really hit it on the head about my parents. The more I thought about it, the angrier I became. It's no fun to be a latchkey kid, even a *loaded* latchkey kid.

I didn't want to spend the rest of the summer doing what everyone else was doing. I wanted to fight dragons and rescue princesses. I wanted to get a life. But I had to have more than a few parlor tricks to convince me to sign up for wizard school. I mean, C-notes don't grow on trees, but it could have been done by sleight of hand.

The mist was swirling thicker and thicker around us, and the sound of the traffic of Ventura Boulevard was like fading into the distance . . . as though we were moving, although I could still feel the sidewalk under my sneakers. "I take it," said Anaxagoras, "that you would like a slightly more sophisticated demonstration of my powers?"

He'd read my mind. Or maybe that's what he said to all his victims. It occurred to me that he might be some kind of mad killer. But no. That didn't jibe with the feeling I had that this was something wonderful, a million-to-one chance that I'd never get again. Still, I didn't want to appear too eager. As my father always says, "You have to read the fine print."

So I'm standing in the middle of the street being offered the secrets of the universe, and I'm all, "Convince me."

"Okay," says the wizard. "We'll do the old dimensional grand tour. Hold on tight for takeoff . . . You don't want to lose your lunch."

16

3

Across the Universe

In a few moments we were totally engulfed in mist and spinning like gyroscopes. I wasn't sure if it was *me* spinning or whether it was the whole world, whirling around me at supersonic speed. "Where are we going?" I screamed.

"Nowhere," said the wizard. "And everywhere. The territory of the soul."

The mist swirled. We broke out of the spin into a soaring arc. The mist streamed past us and I knew we were far above the earth. There were only glimpses of the world beneath. Rolling plains. Castles. Spires that climbed into the sky and were wreathed with rainbows. I didn't recognize any of the places, even though one building bore a passing resemblance to the Wells Fargo Bank on Ventura Boulevard. "So, like, where are we?" I said.

The fog broke for a minute and I could see a rolling

meadow, as green and as clear as an ocean of lime Jell-O. "I think this is Narnia," Anaxagoras said.

"No kidding? You mean like in those C. S. Lewis books?" I hadn't read them, but I *had* caught the miniseries. "But that's not a real place . . . It's a fantasy."

The mist came circling back, and this time when it cleared it was kind of an *Arabian Nights* movie, with minarets and camels and endless desert. Gliding over the rainbow and down the chimney and under the sea. The next time, we were swooping down on a checkerboard landscape, squares of dark and light grass bordered by little creeks. "Don't tell me," I said. "Alice through the Looking-Glass."

"Not bad," the wizard said.

Then to an ice-clad world with crystal rivers crawling to the chunky sea. A world where dinosaurs battled to the accompaniment of Dolby Surround Sound™ Stravinsky. We took in a dragon fight at the mouth of the endless caverns, and we followed the caverns to where the river of forgetfulness circled the mountain of despair. We shrank to the size of amoebas and went microbe hunting in a droplet of water. All right, it was impressive. But maybe it could be done with computers.

We came to rest on the crenelated parapets of Camelot, overlooking a jousting match with horses and ladies in pointy hats and knights in shining armor, the whole bit. The horses pawed the air and I stood there all giddy. Heights aren't my thing.

"Don't worry," said Anaxagoras. "They can't see us."

My stomach gave a little growl. He smiled, waved his hand, and plucked a couple of cheeseburgers out of the air. I munched mine thoughtfully. Although the jousting match was happening right beneath us, in the courtyard, it seemed at the same time to be infinitely far away. The hooves of the horses kicked up dust but made no sound, and they seemed to be moving in slow motion . . . as though we were experiencing a three-dimensional action replay instead of the real events. Yeah. Computers maybe.

"Where to next?" said Anaxagoras. "Don't litter," he added, snatching away the scrunched-up cheeseburger wrapper and making it vanish into thin air. "Into the cosmic recycler," he said.

"Yeah, right," I said. "For all I know, you're dumping the garbage in some vacant parallel universe."

"You'll just have to take my word for it," he said. Then, "Well? What is it to be now? Barsoom? Middle Earth? Atlantis?" He gathered his cloak about his shoulders and did the glowing-eyes trick that usually heralded a major new magic production.

"What about real places?" I said. "I'd really like to know, for instance, what my mom's doing right now. Or how my dad's shoot is going."

"We don't go to real places," Anaxagoras said. "Not yet. You're not ready for the shock of it."

"Maybe you can't really do it."

"Can so."

"So do it."

"No."

"Why not?"

"There's a right way and a wrong way for everything. We must walk before we can run. A stitch in time saves nine."

"You're just throwing off a string of platitudes so I'll get confused."

"That's right. And besides . . . why are you so hung up on the difference between reality and fantasy? Don't you know that life is a dream . . . that the world is an illusion . . . a mirage thrown up by the collective smokes and mirrors of five billion souls? Yes, even the solid and unchanging earth, the sidewalk, the garbage, all these things are there because of magic. Why do you want to know where your parents are? Be happy."

"I can't help thinking that . . . if you really are this all-powerful archmage you seem to be . . . why is it that all you've managed to conjure up for me are a bunch of high-class visual effects? You could have done a lot of this with some kind of virtual reality hookup."

"I'm going easy on you, kid. Now, do you want to sign up for the course or not?"

He pulled a contract out of his sleeve. It was a parchment that just kept unscrolling and unscrolling, and there were miles and miles of fine print, and it all went whizzing by so fast I could barely get through a couple of sentences, all of which sounded pretty ominous. I mean things like: "I, Aaron Maguire, do freely and without coercion apprentice myself to the Archmage Anaxagoras, rendering unto him all the works of my hands and the produce of my mind for a term of five years, extensible unto eternity or the duration thereof if said apprentice fails to reach acceptable standards of high wizardry within said period, said apprentice agreeing to surrender life, limb, free will, independent thought, ego, and choice of fashions to said wizard for entire duration of said period, said wizard agreeing thereto to divulge to said apprentice all pertinent secrets of the universe relevant to the acquisition of such skills of wizardry as said apprentice intends to acquire, subject to the standard disclaimers as to the nature of reality, cosmic perturbations, acts of God, and so on and so forth (see rider on page 2,345,871, paragraph 5, subsection 12b [each fourteen-inch length of scroll being considered for the purposes of this contract as one standard page (foolscap or legal size)])." That was the opening sentence. After that they got too long for me. So I just let the lines of fine print blur past. And then, suddenly, it was all over, and there was just the tail end of the scroll dangling from the wizard's sleeve.

"Sign here," said the wizard.

I laughed. "I'm not going to sign anything," I said. "Not unless my agent looks it over pretty thoroughly first." I didn't have an agent, of course, but I had heard my dad say that over the phone.

The wizard stared into my eyes. It was one of those hypnotic *You will obey* kind of stares. Rings of cold blue light came pinging from his pupils. I had to resist. I could feel the sweat breaking out on my forehead. Pouring down my cheeks. The wizard's eyes kind of stretched out of their sockets and slowly transformed themselves into electric drills, and they were coming right at me, about to jab right into my eyeballs. I was all queasy and squishy with anticipation. I didn't think I could hold out anymore.

Then Anaxagoras started laughing. Big belly bear laugh. He snapped out of his hypnotizing stare. "Well, my boy," he said, "you've just passed another big test. There's absolutely nothing wrong with your bullshit detector. You're in."

"In?"

"Check in at the dojo in the morning for your blue belt," he said, making me wonder if I had just signed up for karate. "Don't worry about how to find the place. It's like the land of Oz; when you have to be there, you will be; and when you don't have to be there, nothing you can do will enable you to make the crossing."

The clouds were gathering again and roiling around us. It was a pity because the jousting was starting to pick up. One of the Sir Lancelot dudes had just been thrown from his horse and this lady in white was swooning. I never found out what happened because we were soon off and soaring again, rewinding our way through all those mythic kingdoms at breakneck speed. That's how I was going to make it to the mall with minutes to spare for the momentous meeting with Penelope—we were slingshoting backward through time. It was cool.

I knew now that I was going to do it. The sorcerer's apprentice thing, I mean. I was an average rich kid with a brilliant mother and an eccentric father, happy in school and contented with his friends, and I lived in the heart of the magic kingdom, but there *was* something missing from my life. It was the magic. It had to be.

But I guess I was still scared to let go, take the big leap of faith, even though the winds of magic were sweeping me back to the shopping mall where my princess waited for me. "I don't know," I said. "Can I trust you? I mean, really trust you?"

I was afraid I'd wake up and still be sitting on the sofa listening to the answering machine . . . and know that I'd dozed off and missed Penelope Karpovsky after all and maybe missed the rest of my life too.

"I see. You want physical evidence. Kid drives a hard bargain."

"Yeah," I said.

So Anaxagoras reaches into his sleeve and the clouds and the shimmering fabric of his cloak are billowing all around us and *bam!* he plucks out a thin flat thing, about the size of a pocket calculator, and he throws it in the air and I watch it flip up and spiral down right into my hand. Feather light. A neon pink frame . . . a mirror. I gazed at it, thinking that it must be some magical item—a window into another universe—a device for zapping people with bolts of blue laser light. But all I could see in it was my own face.

"Keep this for me until we meet again," he said.

"What does it do?" I said.

"Nothing," said the wizard, "unless you know how to make it work. Guard it well, my boy. A lot is riding on what you do with it."

I tucked it into my back pocket. Suddenly we stopped moving. The mist cleared and I was standing on the escalator at the Galleria. "Anaxagoras?" I said. He was gone. If it hadn't been for the mirror in my back pocket, I would have sworn it had all been a dream.

But a telltale smear of smoke hovered in the air about my face.

Well, high fantasy was all very well, but at that moment my hormones started to kick in. Penelope Karpovsky would be waiting for me when I got off that escalator. Maybe the mirror contained some magic that would make her fall head over heels in love with me. There had to be a reason Anaxagoras had given it to me . . . Maybe it was even one of those no-advance-warning tests. Maybe I was supposed to figure out its secret and report back to him at the beginning of next period or I'd flunk out of wizard school before I'd even started. Maybe I was about to be beset by the forces of darkness and unless I could learn its secret I would plunge the entire universe into perpetual bondage of the enemies of light. Maybe it was one of those mirrors that could answer such earth-shattering questions as "Who's the fairest of them all?"

On the other hand, maybe it was just a mirror.

4

Mirror, Mirror

I was a minute early, so Penelope Karpovsky wasn't in front of the pizza place yet. But I could see her standing two door-ways down, gazing soulfully into the window of a jewelry store. I tried to sneak up on her but it was too late; she had seen my reflection in the glass. She was smiling. I didn't look right at her. But in the window, her face shimmered against a back-drop of Rolex watches. She didn't turn to look at me either; she was staring at a five-carat blue diamond at the center of the display.

"Aaron," she said softly. I didn't know what to say. So much had happened in the thirty minutes since I'd heard her voice on my answering machine. I could feel the mirror in my back pocket, rattling against my comb. I looked at her face in the window glass and she was the same girl I'd been attracted to since that day in Mrs. Pepper's biology class when she'd made that joke about xerographic reproduction. I couldn't remember the punch line anymore, only Mrs. Pepper's awed expression. *Nobody* said things like that in Mrs. Pepper's classroom.

"C'mon," she said at last. "Say something. Well, don't say anything if you don't want to. It's okay. Either way. Men who say nothing are fine too. I mean, it's not like I expect you to take charge or anything. I don't believe that men always have to take the lead."

I loved the sound of her voice. "You're pretty into taking the lead yourself," I said.

Then I regretted it, because she looked hurt for a moment. And then she laughed a little. "My shrink says I'm too pushy, like my mother," she told me.

"You have your own personal psychiatrist?" I blurted out. "Your parents must be like majorly rich." I had barely extracted my left foot from my mouth and there went my right.

She looked hurt again—for the barest split second—but then that laugh came bubbling right back up to the surface. "Well, yes," she said, "the parental units are moderately wealthy, by Encino standards. But see, he's like not really *my* shrink, you understand. More like family therapy."

"Divorces and stuff?"

"Everything." She stared off into the distance.

I didn't want to pry, but I could really empathize with her. I mean, I'd watched enough daytime talk shows to know that every "Leave It to Beaver"-like facade of a perfect family has a couple of skeletons in its closet. She was beautiful and she was tragic, which made her about as romantic a figure as you could get. Like Guinevere, like Juliet . . . you know, all those swooning maidens in those legend-type stories. I didn't want to pry, but . . . okay. I *did* want to pry. But, for once, I succeeded in keeping my mouth shut.

She went on, "But I don't want to bore you with my problems. Actually, I don't want to even think about my problems. I want you to sweep me off my feet—you know, a knight in shining armor kind of thing. So you don't have a white horse, but I hear you can do a mean three-sixty on that skateboard. Did you know that I spied on you one time, on the ramp in the Weissmuellers' backyard? You were beautiful. I could have sworn you broke the laws of physics, I mean you just hung there over the edge like a crane with its wings spread against the wind."

I hardly recognized myself in the poetry of that image. "So you want to have pizza?" I said at last.

She giggled. "Sure."

We walked across to Pizza Paradise, which is the sort of nouvelle cuisine pizza parlor that one finds in Encino. We ordered a medium pizza. She had shrimp and avocado on her half; I took the more pedestrian Thai barbecued chicken on mine. She insisted on putting it on her dad's Visa card. We sat down in a booth and she immediately began fussing with her hair. "Oh my God," she said, "do you have a mirror? I mean, I don't want to appear vain or something, but, well, my shrink says that my narcissism is a withdrawal reaction to . . . um, the bad things that happened to me. Actually my self-esteem is totally too low."

It was hard to believe that she could feel at all bad about herself. Again I felt this burning curiosity about her and at the same time this guilt about prying into her problems. She held her hand out for my mirror. A lot of guys keep one in their back pockets. Usually I didn't, but by a stroke of luck I had the mirror the wizard had given me. I handed it over without thinking twice. It was only after it was in her hand that it occurred to me that like, maybe I shouldn't have done that. Because it was a different mirror now. I mean, when I had stuck it in my pocket it'd had a pink neon frame and now it was kind of tortoiseshell and shaped like a heart. And there was a hint of smoke in the air, curling and twirling around the mirror, even though we were in a nonsmoking booth.

Smoke and mirrors. I should've seen the signs.

She's all, "Is my hair okay?" but I'm just sitting there sinking into a puddle of guilt, thinking I'm going to be zapped with a lightning bolt any minute now. I see her looking into the mirror and I see her eyes getting wider and wider. "I can't believe what I'm seeing," she says. "I mean, give me a break, get out of here."

"What are you seeing?"

"No, no, I can't tell you. Can I like borrow this mirror for a few days? I promise, I won't show it to anyone. I totally promise."

"But what's in it?"

"I can't say." But she smiles at me and it's the first time I've ever really seen her smile. No, I mean, she's always smiling, but there's always a hint of sadness in her smile, and that sadness has been wiped away. I crane my neck to try to see the reflection, but there's nothing special. Just her face.

"It's not really *my* mirror. I've got to give it back."

"Oh, please, Aaron. Just a few days. I mean, now that we're going out and all."

How can I resist her? I mean, I think about all those days I spent peering at her in school. She sits behind the grossly overweight Jimmy Matson and the giraffelike Cornelia Quaid, so I only ever get to see Penelope's face when Cornelia leans to one side and Jimmy hunches over to sneak a hit from his stash of Snickers bars. And now she's sitting right in front of me, gingerly wiping the tiny smear of pizza and avocado from the left corner of her lower lip with a dainty fingertip, and she's all "now that we're going out" like it's the most natural thing in the world.

Of course she can borrow the mirror. Of course. She can have anything she wants, as far as I'm concerned. Why shouldn't I flunk out of wizard school? The events of the past half hour are racing through my head, the Camelots, the Narnias, the Atlantises . . . but a little voice inside me keeps saying, *They're not real. This is.* So I tell her, "You can give it back to me next time we meet."

"Tomorrow? But I have family therapy and it puts me in a bad mood all day. The day after tomorrow'd be good."

The mirror belches out a puff of smoke, blacker and thicker than before. There's a whiff of evil in the air. I'm about to warn her, but I don't know what to warn her about. And she's still smiling.

I wish I knew what she was seeing.

Was it telling her, "You're the fairest of them all?" Was it somehow giving her back that self-esteem her shrink told her she was missing out on? Was it flattering her, seducing her somehow?

I didn't care. I just liked looking at the way she smiled.

5

Breakfast

I'm going to have sweet dreams tonight, I thought. But I was wrong. They started out sweet each time but they ended with me waking up, sweating, maybe even screaming.

Like this: I'm standing on the edge of a lake and I'm dressed in shining armor, and it's some kind of *Excalibur*-type fantasy. There are two moons in the sky and a mist-swathed island shimmering on the horizon. And an arm reaches up out of the water just like in those King Arthur books and movies, and it's Penelope—I know because I see her face glimmering beneath the water—but it's not a sword she's holding up to me, it's a mirror with a neon pink frame . . . and I look into the mirror and I see my armor rusting away before my very eyes . . . I see my young body withering and crumbling into the cold, cold water. I can't even call out Penelope's name because I'm all dust now, and my voice is the empty wind.

Or this: I'm skating down an endless ramp and the ramp is mirror metal polished until it dazzles and there's a million me's, distorted by the funhouse curvature of the ramp. Each me is scary as a monster from a slasher movie. I'm skating down, down, down and trying to throw myself into the curve to catch the momentum of the upward arc, except it never curves up, only down and down and down into depths that burn my eyes with the fire of reflected sunset.

Or, or, or . . .

I see Penelope Karpovsky through a kind of blur. She's standing in a marble hallway and looking into a mirror and I am the mirror . . . and she says to me:

> *Mirror, mirror, on the wall,*
> *Who's the fairest of them all?*

But when I start to answer, "You are, of course you are. There's no one else but you," the sound that comes from my throat is a deafening thunder, and she can't understand me . . . and she starts to cry. And I'm all, "Don't cry, Penelope, like, you *are* the fairest of them all, for me, anyway, and I'm the mirror and what I say rules." But the words don't come out, only this roaring, like a volcano, like the smashing surf; she can't hear me; she just goes on crying and then I feel myself being picked up, hurled away, smashed, I feel my glass face splintering into sharp-edged shards across the cold marble floor of the castle.

And then I wake up again.

And the sunlight's streaming in through the miniblinds, and I know that today's the day of my first lesson and I've already flunked the first test by giving away the mirror.

I had no idea how wizard school worked; maybe a bell would go off and I'd suddenly find myself in the classroom. I made my way over to the kitchen, which is in Dad's side of the house. (But it is strictly speaking neutral territory, since they both have to eat.) I fixed myself a huge breakfast of scrambled cholesterol, two slices of broiled cholesterol, and cholesterol on toast. (When Mom is home, cholesterol is banned, but I have a stash of bacon, ham, butter, and all that good stuff in a secret compartment behind the lettuce.)

I wolfed it all down, trying not to think of the ordeal I knew must lie ahead.

Suddenly, my father popped out of the pantry.

"Oh, Aaron, thank God it's you," he said. "I was afraid she'd come home a week early. You know what she's like."

It was true. If he was caught snooping around Mom's side of the house, he was supposed to lose visitation rights for a month. In practice this meant that we could both sit in the living room, on opposing turfs, and converse uneasily while each trying not to look at the other.

Our family was pretty dysfunctional.

"Aren't you supposed to be on the set, Dad?"

"No . . . we're not blowing up the giant kangaroo until after sunset; it's a night shoot." He had a half-eaten ham sandwich in his hand. "You won't tell your mother, will you? I mean about me sneaking into her cholesterol stash."

"Dad, that's *my* cholesterol stash. She doesn't know anything about it."

"Oh, oh. I'll make it up to you. Steak dinner or something."

"When you have time."

He sighed. The phone rang. We looked at each other. It rang awhile longer, and then the answering machine intercepted it. Then we heard a secret code beep intercepting the answering machine. It had to be Mom. My father glanced nervously over his shoulder.

I picked up.

"Hi, Mom."

". . . bzzz . . . seeing a shaman in the hills . . . the price of sapphires . . . bzzz . . . bzzz . . . and, honey, remember only to eat whole grain . . ."

Even through the static of twelve thousand miles, I could tell that my mother was going through one of her phases. Every couple of years, she becomes wildly enthusiastic about some grand and cosmic idea. Sometimes it's a guru; sometimes it's something she reads about in one of those self-help books. I'll never forget the time she became obsessed with the Lüscher Color Test, which is all about understanding your inner nature by your choices of color. She bought seven sets of dinner plates so that we could regulate our mood swings by color-coordinating our eating environment. It didn't work.

"Bzzz . . . luminescence of my inner being . . . and the amulets are such a bargain, let me tell you! . . . Are you brushing your teeth?"

"Yes, Mom, I've already outgrown my dirty-little-boy phase." It never hurts to remind your parents of the obvious.

"Love you, Aaron."

"Love you too. When are you coming back, Mom?"

"Bzzz . . . bzzz . . ." The line went dead, and I watched my father, closing the pantry door behind him, tiptoe out of the kitchen toward his side of the house, still munching on his ham and Wonder bread.

"Are you leaving?" I said. "I thought you didn't have to be on the set until tonight."

"Going to the warehouse to pick up a couple of gallons of Karo syrup. We're all out."

"Splatter night, huh."

"Yeah." Dad sighed and I heard the front door slam and the car start up. I finished my breakfast, carefully eliminated all the evidence down the disposal, and washed the dishes really thoroughly before I stuck them in the dishwasher.

I couldn't call Penelope until tomorrow. I could sit around wallowing in guilt over the mirror, or I could call some of my friends. Somehow I didn't feel like doing that.

I went to the pantry to get some cereal. But when I opened it, it wasn't a pantry anymore. Smoke came billowing out of it. A stairway led down, down, down, to a cavernous vastness that seemed to stretch forever. Somewhere among the stalagmites were the coils of a silver-scaled dragon. The fumes smelled of gasoline and exotic flowers and old incense.

I slammed the pantry shut.

"Go away!" I said.

Then, gingerly, I opened the door again, just a crack. I could see the shelves of spices and cereal boxes. But they were like images painted on a glass wall. Behind them the smoke was roiling and the dragon slithering and there was a weird echoing, like the sound of heavy metal music in a marble bathroom. Then there was like this clanking sound. Footsteps. Metal on stone. Clank. Clank. Someone was coming up the endless steps, coming from the depths of the dungeon.

It had to be Anaxagoras. I couldn't see him yet, but I knew he'd be robed in the majestic vestments of his magic, that he'd probably be waving a big old staff of power at me, and that he would probably be bursting with fury about how I'd given that mirror away less than an hour after it had been entrusted to me. I mean, I've read enough fantasy novels to know that you usually only get one chance to pass the test, and if you happen to fail you are usually beheaded, turned to stone or into a toad, and more or less history.

I tried to close the pantry door again, but this time I couldn't. I pushed and pushed but it wouldn't budge. It was as if there was a whole army on the other side of that door. An army of angry Anaxagorases.

I slunk back to the kitchen table and sat down to await my fate.

The pantry door squeaked as it opened all the way, and I heard Anaxagoras step into the kitchen. I gasped when I saw him. He wasn't wearing any wizardly raiment. In fact, he was wearing an orange jumpsuit and carrying a box of tools.

He tossed me a jumpsuit just like the one he was wearing and said, "Put it on." It was decidedly uncool-looking.

"About the mirror—" I began.

"Yes, yes! Well done! Now put on that thing and we can get on with the first lesson."

"You're not going to punish me for giving away the mirror?"

Anaxagoras only laughed and pointed to the jumpsuit. The shirt pocket had an embroidered logo that read:

ANAXO-ROOTER

Flush your troubles down the drain

"I get it," I said. "It's a disguise."

"Everything we wear is a disguise," said Anaxagoras, "including our bodies. But no, it's not really a disguise. It's pretty practical. You wouldn't want to get your good clothes all filthy where we're going."

"Great!" I said, still hardly daring to believe he wasn't going to kill me over the mirror business. "What are we doing this morning? Slogging through the primeval forest in quest of the dark dragon that's been terrorizing the kingdom? Braving the foul-smelling swamps to rescue the princess from the clutches of a rapacious manticore?"

"Actually, no. We're going down to Mrs. Leibowitz's place on Reseda and Kennedy. Her toilet's clogged."

At that moment I looked out of the window and saw that there was a van parked in our driveway—a green-and-purple van blazoned with the Anaxo-Rooter logo.

"Don't just sit there," Anaxagoras growled in a passable imitation of John Wayne. "We're burning daylight."

I slipped the plumber's uniform on over my skater clothes and grabbed the bag of tools.

"Oh, I almost forgot," the wizard added. He tossed a key

ring onto the kitchen table. There were Yale keys, locker keys, rusty keys, keys to cities, keys for unlocking handcuffs, hotel keys, and crystal keys. "You're driving."

I rooted through the keys until I found one that looked like it might work in the van. "I do have a learner's permit," I said, "so I guess it's okay as long as there's a licensed adult driver in the car with me. . . ."

Anaxagoras began to laugh uproariously. "Licensed!" he shrieked. "Not me. The very idea! I never could get the hang of technology. I don't even know how to use an electric toaster."

It was clear that my first day in wizard school wasn't going to be anything like I'd imagined.

6

Plumbing Lessons

For one thing, I soon realized that we were leaving Encino behind. And it wasn't merely that we were going over the hill, maybe down to Beverly Hills or someplace like that; but instead we turned north, into uncharted territory . . . Reseda . . . perhaps even Northridge. The dark heart of the San Fernando Valley, where the magic of Encino gives way to an endless flat cityscape of shopping malls and tract houses, all frighteningly identical. Of course, that's what the people who live there say about *us*. But, by and large, we do have more money than they do so I guess this is mostly just me being snotty, but . . . but . . . okay.

The plumber's van goes lurching down Reseda Avenue. Even though my driving is not exactly up to my skateboard skills, I manage to keep the vehicle kind of under control.

Reseda and Kennedy was a corner much like any other

corner in the vast wasteland of the central Valley. The house was definitely bourgeois. There were like, gnomes in the garden for God's sake. I lurched into the driveway and narrowly missed knocking one of the gnomes off its pedestal.

"Careful!" said Anaxagoras. "You could have killed it."

"Yeah, yeah," I said.

I got out of the van. "Catch!" He threw me a black bag, kind of like a doctor's bag. Then he disappeared into the van and started tossing out the weirdest collection of tools I'd ever seen. There were like, buzz saws with corkscrews dangling from them, a wooden crown with a gyroscope spinning on top, an astrolabe with flashing lights . . . I didn't particularly try to catch them but they seemed to have some kind of homing instinct because every one of them ended up in my arms and weighing a ton.

So I like staggered into the house and there was this mousy old woman in a floral summer dress standing in the doorway. "In the back," she said. "Oh, I'm so happy you're here; I've only got one bathroom, and—"

"We'll have it all taken care of, Mrs. Leibowitz, don't you worry," said the wizard, "my apprentice and I."

Anaxagoras was all hustling me through the living room and down the hallway toward the back of the house. But, as we reach the bathroom, with Mrs. Leibowitz frantically wringing her hands behind us, and with me lugging a double armful of plumbing gear through Mrs. Leibowitz's shag-piled hallway, somehow it doesn't seem like a very dignified thing for a top-tier wizard to be doing.

"You sweet little boy!" Mrs. L. says, compounding my embarrassment. "You must be such a help to your dear old dad. I'm baking up a batch of cookies, and you'll have one as soon as you're done."

She trotted off to the kitchen, and I looked up at Anaxagoras, who was peering through the tools and discarding one after the other.

"I could have gone skating today," I said.

"You could indeed."

"Aren't I supposed to be learning magic from you? Isn't there some big old book of spells that I'm supposed to recite?"

"Well, yes, all in due course, Aaron. But for now we must direct our attention to this toilet."

"You really mean it, don't you?" To say I was disappointed doesn't begin to describe it.

"I'm afraid I do."

"This is a load of—"

"I'm afraid you're right, Aaron. It is."

"But yesterday you showed me magic kingdoms and fireworks and dazzling spells! Is this some kind of bait-and-switch deal? You sign us apprentices up with a lot of talk about glamour, and actually it turns out we're slave labor?"

"And where, O Aaron Maguire, is the magic mirror I entrusted to your safekeeping?"

Anaxagoras closed his eyes for a moment and the bathroom door shut by itself. The toilet lid—it was covered in some kind of pink fake fur—lowered itself onto the seat and I found myself sitting down and looking up at a stern old man, who all of a sudden seemed like a school principal in a majorly bad mood.

I tried to look solemn. When the principal lectures you, looking solemn helps to like, shorten the agony.

"Now, Aaron, being a wizard is an awesome responsibility, as you know. Magic is what makes the world go round. It is the glue that holds the universe together. Oh, the scientists can talk about electrons and positrons and muons and pions and mesons and gluons and photons and baryons and neutrons and . . . did I say electrons yet?"

"Yes. Electrons and positrons and muons and—"

"Very well. But they're only the physical manifestation of magical forces. The first thing I'm going to teach you is also the only thing I'm ever going to teach you: everything depends

41

on everything else . . . you, young man, are part of an unending chain of being. And that means that if you yank on the chain, you're going to affect everything else in the chain. *Everything.*"

"Sounds like ecology."

"Ecology is a subset of magic."

"Wow," I said. I was, like, interested in spite of myself. I mean, this was totally cosmic. "But I still don't see what it has to do with Mrs. Leibowitz's toilet."

"It has everything to do with it. You see, your mind is up there with the dragons and the unicorns, but the magic that's in ordinary things is the same magic . . . You can't stretch up to touch the stars unless your feet are first firmly planted in the earth . . . That's why I've chosen Mrs. Leibowitz's drain as your first assignment."

"So what do I do? Sort of wave my arms and say a few magic formulas and—presto! it's done?"

"Magic is an art," said Anaxagoras.

And he's all removing tool after tool from the box I carried in. I can't recognize any of them. There's like, an eggbeater with a corkscrew at one end, attached to a crystal sphere with a goldfish swimming around in it. He's all, "No, that's not it." Finally there's something I've seen before in movies: a magic wand. His eyes light up, but he tosses the wand onto the heap. The pile of discarded tools just about fills the whole bathtub.

"How'd you fit all that in the box?" I said, realizing now why it seemed to weigh a ton when I was carrying it in.

"I'm not sure," he said, "it's something to do with folding n-dimensional space. Don't ask me; I don't know anything about physics . . . I just get these gadgets from the mad scientist in the condo next door."

So that wasn't magic either. The last object that Anaxagoras took out was a plunger.

"What's *that* for?" I said.

42

"In case you fail," he said. Then he sat down in the lotus position next to the bathtub and waited for me to act.

What was I supposed to do? I looked blankly at him, and he only raised an eyebrow and said, "Find the connections . . ." and he closed his eyes and seemed to drift away.

I got up and faced the toilet.

I thought about the wizard's big old lecture about the great chain of being and about everything affecting everything else. And all of a sudden I get the feeling I'm not just standing in this place, but I'm like leaking out of myself . . . that the bathtub and the tiles and the sink are somehow blurring into me . . . that we're all melding together. It's a scary feeling and I fight it. I panic and I turn to Anaxagoras for help, but like, he's totally out of it.

I'm not exactly melting, but I think I'm dissolving . . . dissolving as in a movie, when one image slowly fades out and another fades in. I'm a jillion little particles hanging in an Aaron-shaped mist . . . though I haven't moved, my mind is skimming the mirror-smooth tiles, squeaking against the lemony film of bathtub cleaner . . . It's weird but, you know, kind of a cool feeling, tickling, tingling. Now I'm all swirling, like a whirlpool, like the eye of a tornado. What's really strange is, I get the feeling that the tiles, the shower curtain, the sink, are like, my *brothers* or something, that I've got their names on the tip of my tongue, and that like, if I call out to them I can get them to *do* things, I don't know, change their shape or something, because the shape that they are now is an illusion.

So that's the secret . . . or one of them at least. Knowing the names of things gives you power over them. Not the names in English but the names in another language, an ancient one where everything that can be conceived of has a secret and unique name that's known only to itself and the sorcerer who calls it.

Now this knowledge gives me such a head rush, I feel like the most powerful kid in the universe; it's like when you're

shooting up the side of a skating ramp and you suddenly find yourself hanging, upside down, breaking the law of gravity for the splittingest of seconds . . . yeah, it's the same feeling only bigger than that. I think I can do anything at all. Unclogging Mrs. Leibowitz's toilet is the least of it.

I take care of that right away. I reach down there with my mind. I funnel down into the drain and I'm part of the water and I'm surfing on the wave and *being* the wave at the same time. The thing that's blocking the drain's up ahead and its true name comes to me and I call out to it and it shatters into a zillion pieces like the death star or something. I hear the water roaring, I'm standing inside a waterfall, the water's cascading down and making rainbows in the brilliant sunlight and then . . . slowly . . . I start to fade . . . to merge back into my physical self . . . and I know the thundering water is only the flushing of the toilet.

The odd thing is, I'm holding the plunger in my hand.

Maybe I've just been plunging, and maybe the rest of it was just a dream, because I can't seem to hold on to any of the images . . . when I try to grab them they mutate into other images . . . Penelope . . . my dad . . . a king-size chocolate-chip cookie.

"Go on! You deserve it." It's Mrs. Leibowitz, thrusting the cookie into my hand. "Do you take American Express?" she asks Anaxagoras, and he's all, "Sure. It's all the same to us."

The doorbell chimed. Mrs. Leibowitz scurried to open up.

"Quick! Eat up!" said the wizard. He started to throw his equipment into the box. "We have to get out before we're discovered."

"Discovered?"

"Yes. They're here."

"Who?"

"The plumber she called. Come on!"

"You mean she didn't call *us*?"

"Of course not! We're not listed."

"Then what are we doing here?"

"Well, I don't want to spend a lot of time explaining, but strictly speaking, we wizards aren't supposed to practice magic under mundane circumstances . . . but since apprentices have to be taught, one way or another, they tend to turn a blind eye toward this kind of guerrilla wizardry. Still, it wouldn't do to rock too many boats. . . ."

Okay, the next thing that happens is that he spreads his arms wide, and suddenly he's not in his plumber's uniform anymore but in billowing black robes covered with suns and moons and stars, and there's a wind whipping us and his hair's all flying . . . and when I look down at myself I see I'm wearing a white tunic and pointed shoes, the way you'd think a wizard's apprentice should look, and I'm thinking, Now, *this* is fresh, this is how wizardry's all supposed to be . . . And there's a big old peal of thunder and all at once we're out of there, I'm in the driver's seat of the van and backing out of Mrs. Leibowitz's driveway at the speed of light.

"Good job," said Anaxagoras.

"That's it? 'Good job?' I braved the darkness, dude! I fought the demons of chaos and slew the dragon and all! Do I get graded now or what?"

"Hungry?"

We pulled into a burger joint for lunch.

"How do you feel about your first act of magic?" said the wizard as he downed his third vanilla Diet Coke. Well, it was about time he asked me. I mean, like, I'd gotten nothing out of him but grunts and the occasional, "Pass the ketchup."

But now that he asked me, I couldn't really tell anymore. Only a half hour had passed but already the memories had become slippery. I know that it was exhilarating. I know that I felt somehow one with everything . . . that I'd managed to grasp a piece of truth in my hand . . . and that it was already fading from my mind ... "It's like they say about Chinese food," I said. "An hour later you're hungry again."

And it was true. I was hooked.

Hooked on magic!

"It's good to take a long, deep breath before you decide what really happened," Anaxagoras said. "Slaying the dragon, indeed! You'll be slaying them soon enough; and you won't be comparing a dragon to a clogged toilet!"

"Soon? How soon?" This was exciting. I guess I thought slaying a dragon was like some tricky skating stunt, like a 540 ollie or a two-wheel edge carve; you work up to it.

"Calm down."

"You sound like my fifth-grade teacher. She said I was hyper. Wanted them to put me on something."

"I've always found that a vanilla Diet Coke is just the thing," Anaxagoras said, and ordered a fourth one from the waitress.

7

Penelope in the Mirror

When I finally got home, there were half a dozen messages from Penelope Karpovsky on my answering machine. I listened to them all, my pulse quickening each time she said my name. "Aaron, it's me. Aaron, call me. Aaron, where are you? Aaron, like totally call me, Aaron."

It took me a second because I was still coming down from the high of my first bout of magic. I was scared because I knew she had the mirror and I knew I was going to have to face Anaxagoras's wrath about it at some point. I had some wild notion about sneaking to her house, climbing in through the window and jacking the mirror before the next time I saw Anaxagoras. But I had a feeling it wouldn't work. Anyway, in the war between logic and hormones, logic soon fell by the wayside and I picked up the phone, hands trembling a bit, and before it had even rung once I was listening to her voice, and she's all, "Where have you been, Aaron Maguire? I've like, been trying to reach you all day!"

I'm all, "Well, Penelope, duh, uh."

Then it occurred to me that Penelope wasn't supposed to be available today. "Didn't you tell me that you were in family therapy today, and that it'd put you in a bad mood and that like, I shouldn't call you till tomorrow?"

"Well, yes, but . . . I faked a big old PMS attack. I didn't want to go today anyway. Today's the day my mom's New Age guru woman is scheduled to look in on our therapy. I just couldn't face that. Anyways, I want to talk to you about the mirror. Where did you get it from? It's fresh! All my friends want one."

"I don't know," I said. "They're kind of hard to get a hold of."

"One of your dad's big special effects secrets, huh."

She had provided me with a convenient way to lie about the mirror's true nature. "Uh-huh," I said. "And . . ." I added quickly, "I've got to get it back to the studio before my dad misses it."

"Oh . . . are you sure?"

"Well . . . I . . ."

"Well, when are you going there? I mean, I'd *love* to get a look at a real-live effects studio. I've never seen the inside of one before, and—"

I'm really confused now. On the one hand, there's this great new opportunity to impress Penelope with the inner workings of my dad's movie magic . . . and I happen to know that there's something particularly spectacular—the blowing up of a kangaroo—scheduled for tonight. I could just see Penelope's eyes pop at the sight.

On the other hand, the mirror didn't belong to the studio, so I'd have to *pretend* to be returning it somewhere . . . and then retrieve it inconspicuously . . . without having someone from the art department thinking I was walking off with the props or something! It was clearly something that would require all my diplomatic skills to finesse. Could be a lot harder than sorcery, I thought to myself. Then, after taking a deep breath, I'm all, "Sure, Penelope . . . we'll do it . . . there's a big effects scene tonight . . . I'm sure it'll be cool for you to come and watch."

"You're the nicest boy I know," Penelope said. "I'll be right over." She hung up.

I raided the kitchen and made myself a couple of peanut butter, jelly, avocado and bacon sandwiches. Pretty soon the doorbell rang and there she was. She even had her own skateboard under her arm. I didn't even know she skated. "I figured we'd need transportation," she said. I was really glad because I'd been wondering how I was going to tell her that I didn't have a car or even a license.

"Do you have the mirror?" I said.

She's all, "Yeah, of course I do," but all of a sudden she's looking at the floor and I have a strange suspicion that she doesn't want to give it up.

"Let me have it, then."

"Well, but let me hang on to it for just a little while, okay? I mean, it is *such* a cool mirror. The things you can see in it! What is it, some kind of LCD screen? But the colors are so *vibrant,* it must be like twenty-four-bit."

"Yeah," I said, "twenty-four-bit. That's right." My curiosity was driving me insane now. "Shall we go?"

I grabbed my own board and we coasted downhill to Ventura Boulevard . . . then we turned west and skated serenely toward Tarzana, weaving easily through scattered pedestrians . . . little old ladies walking their dogs . . . shoppers emerging from yuppie emporia . . . watching the endless stream of Porsches, BMWs, and silver Japanese cars go by . . . into the sunset. Penelope squeezed my hand. We skimmed along in a kind of slow-motion slalom. It was almost as though we were at sea.

"Smooth sailing," Penelope said, almost reading my mind.

It dawned on me that there *was* something magical about how we could hardly feel the bumps and cracks in the sidewalk. It was at that moment that I happened to look down. We were a good half inch *above* the sidewalk. We were literally floating. Nervously, I glanced at Penelope, but she was skating with her eyes closed. I let go of her hand a moment and she immediately made contact with the concrete and she let out a little gasp; I seized her hand once more and she was on air again.

And all this time I'd thought I was just an exceptionally good skater . . . I had never realized that I had a completely different gift. Yeah! It was magic, all right. I felt a sense of oneness with the board, with the trucks, with the concrete . . . the same feeling I'd gotten when I sent my mind funneling down Mrs. Leibowitz's toilet . . . the feeling of knowing a thing's true name.

A telltale wisp of smoke tendriled up from around my sneakers. I've got the talent all right, I thought. I bet I could do *anything* if I put my mind to it . . . anything old smoke-and-mirrors Anaxagoras can do.

It was starting to get pretty dark by the time we reached the old warehouse where Dad was working on this movie. I could tell from the catering truck parked outside. The place looked exactly like three other warehouses in the same lot, which were all furniture storage places; if you didn't know where to look, you'd never have known there was a movie being shot in the neighborhood. We walked right in. There was someone guarding the door, but they never ask any questions if you look like you belong there.

We checked our skateboards with the security dude and then I gave Penelope the grand tour; not that I'd visited this

52

actual set before, but they're all pretty much the same. It's pretty easy to orient yourself.

First off I took Penelope to craft services so we could get something to drink, and then I set off to look for Dad. No one really noticed us. All the sets for the movie were crammed right up against each other with narrow corridors of scaffolding between that you could barely squeeze through. I showed Penelope the Egyptian tomb set but we couldn't get inside because it was cordoned off with a "hot set" sign. Penelope said, "What does that mean?"

"Just that the continuity people will have a spaz if some minor little prop has gotten shifted between shots, so they don't want anyone in here snooping and moving things around." My knowledge made a gratifying impression on her.

"Any big stars around?"

"Not really. It's a pretty low-budget affair. Not *quite* as bad as *The Beast That Threw Up Schenectady*, but only a couple of million. You might see Tygh Simpson, the lead singer from the Senseless Vultures. He's doing a cameo. Ever since his album bombed last year, he's been trying to make a comeback by appearing in movies."

"Cool!" I knew that the best way to keep her all shivery with excitement was to act totally nonchalant about the whole thing. At that moment, we emerged from one of the tunnel-like aisles, between the monster's cave and the mad professor's secret hideout, and Tygh himself came whizzing past, followed by a wardrobe person who was trying to straighten his hairpiece. "Oh my God," said Penelope. "That was *him!*"

"Stay cool, Penelope," I said.

"I guess I'm kind of acting too much like a tourist, aren't I?" She calmed down.

We went into the same corridor we'd seen Tygh disappear down, and we could tell by the blinding lights and the sounds of activity that we were coming up to where they were actually shooting. The set was a hotel bedroom; two walls of it were up. Where the other two walls should have been, there were a couple of dozen people working: some grips laying down a dolly track for the camera, a sound man, the director deep in conference with Tygh, and the makeup effects people—my dad and four of his assistants, fiddling with an enormous stuffed kangaroo. Several other kangaroos stood in the background.

"Great!" I said. "They *are* gonna do the exploding kangaroo sequence now."

"Why do they have so many of them?"

"I think each kangaroo is only good for one shot," I said. "I mean, like, they *are* blowing them up. That's a pyro guy over there," I added, pointing to this big dude I've often seen on sets; the last time was *The Day New York Blew Up into Itty-Bitty Pieces*, which was precisely what he had been hired to do. I showed Penelope how he was all setting the charges on the kangaroos. It was cool.

Dad saw me and waved us over.

"Don't mention the mirror," I whispered. "I wasn't supposed to have it."

"Okay."

Dad seemed pretty distracted. His assistants were bustling around making the final adjustments on the kangaroo; he barely paid attention to them. And Penelope's all, "What are they doing?" and I was trying to explain the intricate details of Animatronics to her . . . the different wires and levers used to animate the kangaroo . . . the tubes that led to vats of blood-red Karo syrup that were probably going to spray the set with ersatz gore.

"It's like *magic!*" she said.

But I said, "Nothing to it, Penelope . . . just smoke and mirrors, is all. Which reminds me that I ought to get that mirror back from you so I can . . ."

"Oh, all right, Aaron. But you're such a spoiler." She reached into a pocket and pulled it out. I breathed a sigh of relief when I actually saw it. A little hastily, I reached out for it, but at that moment we were interrupted by my dad, who'd finally seen us and was coming over. Quickly, Penelope pocketed the mirror again. I couldn't very well explain that there was actually nothing to hide . . .

"This wasn't such a great time for you to come visit the set," Dad said. "Fact is, we're having a bit of a crisis."

"Wow, a crisis!" Penelope said. "I watch 'Entertainment Tonight' all the time . . . I *love* it when they have a crisis on the set, it's cool. You mean, like, the heroine stalking off to her trailer in a huff and the producer banging on the door trying to get her to come back to the set and the union getting mad and. . . ."

Dad laughed a wan laugh. "Hardly," he said.

She's all, "Okay, then . . . you're way over budget and the financiers are about to show up with an armful of cooked books? Or maybe a sex scandal. Or a plagiarism suit, like when Art Buchwald sued about that Eddie Murphy movie . . . that was fresh."

Dad finally laughed out loud. "No, it's a lot more mundane than that. It's this sleazy warehouse they rented for this shoot . . . as of an hour ago, all the drains are clogged up . . . it's a monster of a clog . . . a clog as big as the Ritz-Carlton Hotel I bet! And the only toilet that's working is in Tygh Simpson's trailer, and you know how touchy stars can get."

At that moment, a dude in an Armani suit came waddling through, barking into a cellular phone. "A plumber, a plumber, my kingdom for a plumber!" he said. "What do you mean, you can't get here for another two hours?"

Penelope and I looked at each other. "The producer," we both said at the same time.

"Yes . . . there's a line a mile long to go to the bathroom, and the exploding kangaroo probably won't go off until midnight," said my dad, sighing.

It was at that moment that I realized that I, alone among all these great experts, had the power to save the day. "Dad," I said, "I don't want to sound all full of myself, but I do believe I can fix that toilet."

8

A Little Movie Magic

W hich was, you might think, a rather foolhardy thing to say. But, as it happened, I *did* fix the drain, in the first unsupervised, intentional, and 100 percent effective magical act of my career.

It was a very poorly equipped warehouse, but on the other hand, I suppose that it was never intended to house twelve sets and a hundred egomaniacs. Big crates rarely have to go to the bathroom, so the facilities were limited and primitive—there was one dingy, grungy room at the very end of a cave of dripping slime (tinfoil and the ever-present Karo syrup).

"What," said Dad, "makes you think that *you* can fix the plumbing around here?" He gave me the kind of stare that made me all too aware that he still remembered the time I'd tried to fix the espresso machine. Our much-beloved dachshund, Kielbasa, developed such a morbid fear of coffee since that time, we had to give him to a friend of ours in Santa Monica, a Zen therapist-shaman who only drinks ginseng tea.

"Well, like, I can't explain, Dad, but recently I've been given some, like, profound insights into the true nature of plumbing."

I expect Dad to roll his eyes and tell me to get lost, but instead he looks at me quite seriously, almost as if he knows more than I think he knows, which is impossible . . . isn't it? But then again, if I *am* as talented at wizardry as they say, maybe I've done a little unconscious bending of reality to make him see things my way, because suddenly he's all, "Well, son, you see what you can do; there's nothing to lose, not while we're standing around waiting for someone else to get up and do something. . . ."

"Okay," I said.

I asked Penelope and my father to wait outside.

"Need any tools?" Dad said.

"No. Can't explain," I said. "Trade secrets."

"I understand," said Dad, and I'm sure he totally did, since he was in the middle of a lawsuit against Stupendous Media Magic Industries, who had stolen his process for making giant bugs fly without wires, a process he developed in working on the movie *Darling, I Decapitated the Dog.* "Sure you don't need any tools?"

"Nuh-*uh.* I just, uh, 'vaant to be alooone.' "

Dad turned to Penelope and said, "I gotta warn you about this kid; he's crazy; I love him to death, but he's a maniac."

Once alone, I concentrated hard, trying to get my mind back into the state it was in in Mrs. Leibowitz's house. I knew that there were no magic words or mystic gestures to be made. Spells could help to get you into the right frame of mind, but they couldn't compare with making contact with the animate essence of Nature herself. I sent my mind spiraling out of myself . . . I could see it, like a neon whirlwind, whooshing around in the must and mildew. It was a lot easier to detach myself this time, because I knew what to expect. But this wasn't like Mrs. Leibowitz's. I could tell right away that the problem was much greater.

I don't mean that it was because there was more stuff down this drain than the other drain. I mean that, when I sent my mind flying down into the depths, I ran into a *thing* that didn't want to budge . . . a *thing* with a mind of its own. I didn't know what it was, didn't understand it . . . but well, like, have you ever stared at yourself in a mirror, stared at your own eyes, stared so hard that your face starts to transform into like a monster face and you realize the most terrifying thing in the world is yourself? . . . No? Try it sometime. There I was funneling through the swirling, murky waters and trying to blast my way through the barrier of mud and decay . . . and there was this other thing there too, like a prickle of unease always at the back of my mind, and I charged on straight down through the churning water, scared to look back in case I'd come face-to-face with the distorted mirror image of myself. This wasn't a joyous, triumphant magic, not like the first time.

I was fighting a monster, but I didn't dare look at the monster's face. It wasn't just a huge and formless mass of sludge. It was alive. It coiled and coiled around me like a dragon, and I didn't have any weapon I could kill it with. Its breath smelled of garbage and gasoline. I could hear it slithering through the caverns of my mind. I could hear its heartbeat.

"Get away!" I said. I was groping to find what name to call it so it'd leave me alone. Maybe it was breathing fire but all I could feel was cold and clammy and the feeling of drowning and not being able to claw my way back up to the surface. But I knew I had to turn, had to confront it, had to banish it.

I screwed up all my courage. I whirled and swirled. *Be the wind,* I told myself. *Blow him away.* I was just on the verge of turning to face the dragon when, all at once, I couldn't sense its presence anymore.

No. Only a hint of mocking laughter behind the churning of the waters. Then that too was gone, replaced by the whisper of waters.

"Come back!" I screamed at last. "Come back and fight." But it only faded away. I thought I heard the darkness speak softly, "Later. When you're ready for me, boy."

Suddenly I knew that something had been taken from me. You know that feeling you get when you open your locker and someone's been rifling through your things. Or when you're on a vacation in Cancún or somewhere, and your parents have gone off to their yuppie pleasures, and you're all wandering alone through the marketplace and suddenly you realize your wallet's gone. You feel all empty and you don't know why—violated.

Something was missing. I don't know what. But I suspected that the dragon had robbed me of a little piece of my soul. Was this feeling, this desolation, the hidden price of my newfound talent? If it was, I didn't know if it was really something I wanted to go on with.

Oh God, I was confused. Maybe, if I did a *really* big piece of magic, I'd lose so big a chunk of myself that I wouldn't know myself anymore.

Then, all at once, my mind came racing back into my body like a turtle retreating into its shell. I snapped out of the hyperreality of magic and found myself back in the bathroom, which was full of smoke. I coughed. The door swung open and I could see, through a gap in the smoke, Penelope, standing in the doorway, gazing intently at the mirror, not paying attention at all to the world around her.

"Penelope," I shouted, "don't look at it too much—" Because I couldn't understand its hold over her, and I was starting to be scared it would do something bad to her, like steal her soul or something . . . and, startled, like she'd been caught

60

shoplifting or something, she guiltily stuffed the mirror back into her pocket.

The smoke was condensing into a rainbow-fringed mist.

The sound of flushing toilets filled the air.

I stepped out of the bathroom to a burst of applause. Everyone was there—from the producer down to the dolly grips—and they were all clapping like crazy. Even Tygh was grinning, which didn't go too well with his Gothic rock look, which was the flavor of the month in Valley chic. I blinked, then like, the smoke cleared.

The producer's all, "Brilliant!" although he doesn't talk to me directly but to my dad. "How does he do it?"

"A family secret," Dad says. He winks at me. I've never heard of our family being known for its toilet-fixing abilities, but I play along.

The producer looks at me and says, "I suppose I'll have to reward your son somehow, considering he's just saved us a few thousand in lost time . . ." He's obviously the kind of dude who is so used to addressing people *through* other people that he can't actually say anything to anyone directly . . . weird. "What do you think he would like?"

He's just like one of those kings in those fairy tales, you know, the ones who say: "Thou hast rid my kingdom of the fearsome dragon; ask any boon, and you shall have it," at which the handsome, buff, and modest young hero is supposed to reply, "The hand of your daughter, O King, and half your kingdom, and a brand-new Porsche."

"A Porsche, eh?" said the producer, and everyone gasped, including me. I hadn't meant to say that aloud. I guess I was so absorbed in the dragon-slaying fantasy, it was kind of carrying me along.

"Oh, no," I said quickly—Dad's face was rapidly turning purple with embarrassment—"I meant . . . a horseshoe. Yeah, I collect them. Lucky, you know. Magic. They're cool." I wasn't fooling anyone for a moment.

"Well," said the grateful monarch, "I do have an old one I was about to throw out. I'll have it delivered to your house first thing."

Did he mean a Porsche or a horseshoe?

The producer didn't bother to clarify his statement. He pulled out his cellular phone and began punching buttons. The crowd broke up and everyone went back to work. Over the next hour, they blew up four kangaroos. Or maybe more, but once you've been on a shoot, you realize that it's incredibly boring; all people do is stand around waiting for something to happen. Well, even for Penelope, who was having a serious case of tourism at first, it got unglamorized pretty quick.

In fact, after we watched the shoot for a decent interval, she couldn't wait to pull me away from there. She tugged my arm and we found ourselves back at craft services, helping ourselves to the remains of the catering. Even at eleven at night, the table was still piled high with half-eaten chocolate cakes, sides of salmon, turkeys, and potato chips.

She waited until there was absolutely no one around, and then, urgently, she's all, "Stop lying to me, Aaron. There's something going on and you're not letting me in on it."

"You wouldn't believe me."

"Why did you start mumbling about slaying a dragon and getting a boon from the king? Are you stuck in some kind of role-playing game, like those kids on the news who laid siege to the Sherman Oaks Galleria?"

"No, no, it's nothing like that." But I was still worried about why I'd said all that aloud. I had to get a grip on the magic before it started to get a grip on me. "I'm in control, thanks. Really."

"Good," she said, "though it would've been cool to have you in therapy with me."

"I'm not trapped inside my fantasies or anything like that." I wasn't sure I could trust her, but I had come to the conclusion that I had to tell someone. I was badly shaken even though I was trying hard to appear cool. It's not every day that you are chased by a dragon in the sewers of Tarzana. "Look," I said, "that mirror . . ."

"Oh, can I keep it?"

"Well . . . I . . ."

"It's just about the cleverest thing I've ever seen. I mean, every other mirror I know shows me as being a fat slob, but this one—"

"Oh, Penelope, you're *not* a flat slob!" I said. "You've told me that you have a problem with self-esteem, but . . . I've got to tell you this . . . you're totally beautiful."

She only laughed a little. "Let me keep the mirror," she said.

"Well . . ."

"Till tomorrow. No one's going to miss it." She started walking toward the exit; the mirror was still in her pocket, and I began loping after her, taking big strides and having a hard time keeping up.

"All right. But there's something I've got to tell you."

"I love secrets." She picked up her skateboard and the guard opened the door for us. "So like, tell me! You've been working on a new variant of a backside air-to-fakie. Gonna name it the Maguire."

"No, it's nothing like that," I said.

"Um . . . you're really twins, and I've been going out with the other one all evening without knowing it?"

"No, actually it's just that I'm a sorcerer's apprentice," I said.

"Coolness!" she said. "Do you want to go to a movie on Friday?"

9

Suspending Disbelief

O kay, so, like, she didn't believe me.

That much was clear. I didn't mention it again as we coasted home down the boulevard in the neon night. She told me about what her parents do for a living, about her sister who's working at the William Morris Agency, about her aunt Elizabeth, you know, of the Elizabeth line of cosmetics . . . I only listened with half an ear. I mean, I was still captivated by being close to her and by the way her voice sounded, but I was also tormenting myself over what had really happened at the set.

We'd only gone about a half mile when Dad pulled up alongside us.

"Got the rest of the night off," he said, rolling down the window. "I bet you guys want a ride home."

I didn't feel like it at all, but Penelope smiled and said,

"Oh, thanks, Mr. Maguire," and Dad said, "Call me Beau," and smiled right back. I ended up alone in the back of the BMW, and she and Dad started up an intense conversation about channeling. Turned out her mom and my mom had once been in the same channeling workshop down in Santa Monica, before the guru running the show had been turned in for sexually harassing his clients.

Penelope's voice was music to my ears, of course, but sometimes it's better to listen to background music than to have it be the center of attention; I sat in the back thinking about magic. I realized now that Anaxagoras wasn't going to write a bunch of spells on the board and have me memorize them—it wasn't like Mrs. Hernandez teaching Spanish verbs. I was going to have to learn everything by doing it. I was going to have to pick up what I could, on the fly, keeping my eyes and ears peeled, dissecting every one of the wizard's utterances to glean whatever insights I could into the way magic worked.

We were pulling into our driveway, and I realized that I hadn't even noticed Penelope getting dropped off. I couldn't believe myself. What was wrong with me?

"I'd better go to sleep," Dad said. "Tomorrow's call is before the crack, and it's all the way up in Valencia. You should go to bed too. I know people don't turn into pumpkins anymore, but it *is* after midnight, and don't you have school or something?"

"Dad . . . it's *summer*."

"Summer school, then. I seem to remember something about . . . flunking geometry, was it?"

I gulped. It was true. I *was* supposed to start tomorrow . . . only for two hours a day, but still, what a downer. I'd managed to forget all about it, what with whizzing down Milagro, running into the wizard, meeting Penelope at the mall, even the plumbing . . . I mean, school seemed like a total anticlimax.

"Can you write me a note?"

"A note? And why, pray? It seems a little frivolous."

"Dad—the cholesterol police might just decide to Reveal All."

"You can't get me on that . . . your mother's in Thailand with some shaman, remember? And besides, you seem to forget that she and I aren't talking." The garage door whirred and we were pulling in.

"I wish you'd stop fighting."

"We *have* stopped fighting, Aaron. I think we're coexisting pretty well now that we've drawn the line through the middle of the house. As for getting back together . . . well, we just don't see eye to eye, you know that."

"But, Dad—"

"The magic's gone away, son. I don't know if there ever *was* any magic. But what do you know of love?"

"A lot," I said, "I'm sixteen."

"Yes," Dad said, and he was laughing a little, like a joke I didn't get, "yes, you are."

We were inside, and Dad was shambling across to his side of the house. Although it was still Dad's turn to have custody, I decided to sleep on Mom's side of the house. Usually, when I know I'm going to have a bad night, I find Mom's side more soothing. It doesn't smell of glue and latex, but of lemon and Pine-Sol.

But as soon as I set my alarm, draw the blinds, undress and lie down, the bad dreams start.

I'm in the Arthurian place again. There are the islands swimming in the mist. There's the Lady of the Lake rising out of crystalline water and her hair all flaming, holding the sword . . . and there I am, my frail body weighed down by a ton of armor . . . not medieval armor but a kind of thrash metal concoction, all spikes and chains and studded leather . . . reaching out for the sword . . . an eerie, high-pitched music, like a New Age tape played at superspeed, echoes in the air. The colors are totally saturated; it's a movie reality, not the real world . . . it's beautiful but there's danger. I can smell it. I reach out to touch the sword and—

It shatters and—

Where the sword once was there's a mirror and the mirror is framed in curlicues of gold, but I can't see my face in the mirror because of the smoke that spews up from the churning water and—

The Lady of the Lake has Penelope's voice and she's all laughing at me and saying, over and over, *"I don't believe you I don't believe you I don't believe you . . ."* and I'm shouting, "I *am* a sorcerer, I am, I am—" but my shouting is swallowed up in her mocking laughter and—

I woke up. It was totally dark. The bed was making me seasick. "Waterbeds," I told myself, "that's all it is." I slipped out of bed, tiptoed through the dark house, felt my way along the corridor in Dad's side of the house until I reached my other bedroom, the one with the glow-in-the-dark latex decapitated head from *The Swallow That Swallowed Texarkana.* At least the phosphorescent eyes provided some kind of light.

I closed my eyes and recited a calming mantra that Mom had once picked up from her guru and tried to teach me. I don't know exactly when I fell asleep because the transition was gradual . . . I was rocking back and forth and it occurred to me that I wasn't in bed, I was lying on planks on a kind of Viking ship that was all tossing in the wind. Although I was in the middle of the ocean—I couldn't see land—the tempest smelled of sewage and pollution. Far away I could see the lady holding up the mirror, and the light from the mirror burned on the water . . . suddenly I realized that this lake or sea or whatever it was was whirling around and around the lady and the mirror . . . like an emptying drain . . . If I couldn't snatch away the mirror, I'd be sucked down into the depths and drown . . . and then I saw, jutting here and there out of the turbulence, the thousand gleaming coils of the dragon I had failed to fight . . . the dragon whose face I hadn't dared look at . . . the dragon that might well have been my own inner darkness.

That's when I *really* got scared.

I screamed. I woke up. It was like, three in the morning. I looked at the eyes of the latex head . . . the eyes were glowing . . . and then, all at once, I felt the bed rocking again, this time it seems that the whole house is moving, shifting . . . *Oh my God,* I'm thinking, *I'm stuck in this dream and I can't wake up* . . . and then I hear lights and sirens, and behind the closed blinds, there's like a strobe light flashing kind of thing, and then the decapitated head falls off the chest and rolls around on the floor, and I sit up in bed just in time to hear my dad, who's shouting, "Wake up, wake up, it's an earthquake!"

So I spring out of bed the way I've been trained to, and I run to the front door, which is open, and Dad's already there; we're both standing under the doorway, in our underwear, looking very, very disoriented.

"This is terrible," Dad said, as the rolling subsided. "It must be like about a six-point-three or so."

But I'm all, "Thank God it's only an earthquake."

Earthquakes I could handle. After all, this *is* Los Angeles. It's the other stuff—whirlpooling oceans and ladies with magic mirrors and dragons that coil and coil and coil around the sea—*that* stuff is difficult to take.

Earthquakes have a way of bringing me back to reality. I realized that I was too tired to think straight, so I crawled back into bed and slept like a log.

When morning came it seemed like I really *had* crossed over into a fantasy universe. Well, in the first place, there was a message from Penelope on my machine. "You're probably not awake yet," she said, "but I am because, guess what, I have summer school. Forgot all about it until I saw the note on the refrigerator when I got home. I *hate* geometry!" Well, this wasn't exactly bad news; at least I'd be seeing her every day.

But the most amazing thing of all was—there was a Porsche parked in the driveway with a big blue ribbon tied around it and a card with the Stupendous Pictures logo on it that said, "For the master plumber." Well, like, of course it wasn't *new* . . . in fact it looked like about a 1972 . . . and the red paint had gotten a little funky over the years . . . and there was, like, dust half an inch thick over every square centimeter of it. Even so, not the kind of thing you'd casually toss into the Dumpster, although the producer's neighborhood probably boasted a better class of garbage than ours.

I didn't have a license, of course. I'd driven the wizard's van, which wasn't exactly legal since I was supposed to have a *licensed* driver in the car; but on the other hand, since he *was* a wizard, I was sure he could have magicked us out of danger if danger had threatened. On the *other* hand, what was the point of having wheels if you couldn't brag about them to someone? And how far was it to school anyway? Only a mile up the hill . . . and I didn't have to go onto the boulevard . . . or take the freeway . . . or anything like that. Should I or shouldn't I? It was like there was a little horned dude whispering in one ear, and the other dude with the wings and halo wagging his finger in the other.

Okay, so I'm not perfect. The temptation was just too much. I threw my skateboard and my books on the passenger seat, got in, turned the key in the ignition . . . and drove the winding mile up toward Mulholland, to the parking lot of Claudette Colbert High School, without incident. Still, I was sweating when I walked into class fifteen minutes early, especially since I saw that Penelope was there . . . and that she was surrounded by a bevy of blondes—it seemed as though everyone in the entire universe had failed geometry—and was talking about *me*!

She didn't see me, but she's all, "And he took me on to

this movie set where they had, like, this Animatronic kangaroo that totally blew up . . . and then he fixed the toilet and the producer promised to give him a Porsche as a reward . . . oh, and he's so cute . . . a total Clydesdale."

I can feel myself starting to blush.

"Doesn't he have *any* faults, Karpovsky?" says Amanda Hathaway, a lanky girl with *Alien*-looking braces.

"Well . . . he can be kind of uninvolved sometimes. Like he's on another planet, you know? And, like, really *weird* things just pop out of his mouth. Last night, we were just talking normally, and suddenly he's all, 'I'm a sorcerer's apprentice.' "

"Like Mickey Mouse in *Fantasia*?" says Buffy Margarita, the couch potato of the group, with the paunch to prove it.

"I don't know. But I'm all pretending I didn't hear it. I mean, why embarrass him? He doesn't know he does it. Maybe he'll accidentally say some deep secret and I can, like, blackmail him."

The girls are all laughing their heads off when Buffy suddenly notices me and she actually screams, like the lady in *Psycho*.

"I'm not *that* scary, am I?"

Penelope's all embarrassed for a moment, but then she steps away from the other girls, takes me by the hand, leads me toward my seat. "But seriously," she says, "you're not really a sorcerer's apprentice, are you? I couldn't stop thinking about it all night. I thought maybe you meant, since your dad is like, a 'wizard of effects,' that he's been teaching you all his tricks."

I smile in what I hope is a mysterious and not too doofus-like fashion, and I'm all, "What if I told you I was? Would you like, believe me?"

"I like make-believe. The therapist is always making us do make-believe sessions, and I'm the only one in my family who can do it without getting all embarrassed."

71

"Well, but this is more than make-believe. This is make-believe so hard it's more real than real reality." I'm losing her. Actually I'm losing myself, too, because the logic's getting twisteder and twisteder. She looks at me like I'm a thing in a zoo and I say, "Well, but the mirror. The mirror proves it, doesn't it? And by the way, can I have it back now?"

"It's in my locker."

"Can we go and get it? I really need it. Something terrible will happen if I can't give it back—"

"Oh, a curse? Cool!" she says. For a moment I think she's going to torture me some more, but instead she leads the way—with three minutes to go before the start of class—and we go down the hall toward the lockers.

A minute later I'm holding the thing in my hand. What's it all about? Why does it exert such a powerful pull over Penelope, so that she's so reluctant to give it back? Right now she's still touching it, not wanting to let go, and I think she's even starting to cry maybe.

I want to see what's in the mirror. It scares me. It has something to do with the nightmares I've been having . . . and something to do with the dragon that lurks in the sewage system of Los Angeles . . . and something to do with myself. It's calling to me. And it wants to suck me in. Pull me down the drain and flush me away. What is this dragon and why does it keep gnawing at the back of my mind? Why doesn't Penelope seem to be frightened at what's in that mirror? Is what you see in it different for every person? I'm scared for her, and the way she holds on to it is fierce and desperate.

"Let go," I say, and I sound kind of brusque and I regret saying it that way, but it's too late and I snatch the mirror out of her hands and turn it around to look into it and—

That's when the whole corridor seems to fill with smoke, and everything goes all blurry, and I feel the wizard's gnarled hand on my shoulder, pulling me backward into some wild, kaleidoscoping place. . . .

10

In the Wizard's Lair

After a quick "Huh? What? Where?" I landed hard on my behind on a cold and stony floor. This looked like some kind of a cave, with stalactites and stalagmites and a dank odor, and a stream that wound its way among the limestone columns. There were shelves carved into the walls and I saw leather volumes and stuffed rats, bats, and snakes. "Anaxagoras!" I screamed, and I heard the echo go *Xagoras-goras-oras-ras-as-sssss* around and around me. I felt behind me with the hand that wasn't holding the mirror, touched something mushy . . . turned, yelped in shock at the sight of a human skull half covered in some kind of goo.

Anaxagoras materialized in a shimmer of rainbow light.

"But—that's a human skull!" I said. Maybe he wasn't a wizard after all . . . maybe he was the kind of dude who kills people and keeps their body parts in a secret hiding place . . . I had to admit I was terrified.

73

"Human skull, eh?" he said, laughing. He picked the thing up and put it back up on one of the shelves. "Your wizard-sense must be a bit off today."

I took a good look at it. "Oh," I said, realizing what it was from the telltale serial number painted on the jawbone. "It's one of *those* skulls."

"I'm sorry," he said. "I just couldn't help myself . . . cruising through your father's studio. I didn't think he'd miss just *one*."

"It's okay. They used four thousand, three hundred seventy-one fake skulls in that movie, *The Skulls That Couldn't Stop Grinning*. Dad gives them away all the time. He means to throw them out, but . . ." Stupid of me. I always babble too much when I've been made to look like a total dweeb. I stopped myself and handed back the mirror. "Here it is," I said sheepishly. "I forgot to give it back to you before."

"So what did you think of it?"

"Think of it? I—uh—"

"The mirror."

"I—"

There was an eerie glow about his eyes. I backed away. He knows, I thought, *he knows*, and he's just allowing me to dig my own grave and jump in. But instead, he simply tossed it back to me. I grabbed it—it was ice-cold—and stuffed it in my back pocket. "Talk to me when you've learned how to use it," said Anaxagoras. "For now, I want you to get acquainted with my lair. You're going to be spending a lot of time here. . . ."

"Wow," I said. I wasn't quite as awed as I'd been before.

"You'll come and go when the need arises," said Anaxagoras. "I'm sure you'll figure out how it's done. And don't worry . . . There is no time here. Time stands still. This means . . . that if you can't get your wizardry exercises done properly, you'll simply remain here until they *are* . . . understand? For all eternity, if necessary."

"Oh," I said, "kind of like detention."

"You got it! Now, the first lesson of the day . . ."

Anaxagoras launched into this long old spiel about the unity of mass and energy, the oneness of time and space, the mutability of matter, and the stretching of the fabric of the universe to encompass multiplex realities. I must have yawned or something or maybe even totally zoned out because the next thing I knew, he was tapping me on the forehead with his star-studded magic wand. "Your eyes are glazing over," he said.

"They sure are. This is *worse* than summer school geometry! Do I really have to know all this stuff?"

"Nah," he said. "You're a natural."

"What does that mean?"

Suddenly he became all serious. He put his arm around my shoulder and said, "Do you know how many years of study it took me before I had enough magic in me to unclog a simple toilet?"

"But . . . that was kind of easy. I mean, I just sent my mind flying down the pipes and . . ."

"My son, my son . . ." He waved his arms and two beach chairs appeared, enabling us to sit down. "The detachment of the mind from the body usually comes around, oh, fourth year or so. Let's face it: You're kind of an idiot savant when it comes to magic."

"Like the retarded dude who knew how to, uh, find the square root of a hundred-digit number even though he couldn't remember his own name?" I'd seen something about that on "Sixty Minutes."

"Yes," he said. "That's why you're such a precious gift to us, and why you're so . . . so dangerous. And why I've elected to take on your case myself." It was the first time he'd really let slip that he wasn't just any old wizard, but some kind of exalted multi–black-belt wizard dude way high in the wizard hierarchy. "Oh, what am I to do with you?"

"Teach me how to turn lead into gold and stuff . . . or dollar bills into C-notes."

"Even I can't do that."

"But I saw you—"

"No. That was an illusion. But to change the very nature of things . . . the essence of their being . . . that is an arduous thing, indeed, and it's your special gift to be able to do that casually, without even understanding the theory of it." He winked, and our deck chairs transformed themselves into leather easy chairs, and then to expansive hammocks slung across the stalagmites, rocking us gently to and fro.

"For example," he said. "These hammocks we're sitting in . . . are they real?"

"What do you mean?" And then I understood what he was saying. Because my mind . . . the inner *me* . . . it kind of flexed itself, leaned against the canvas, and what it felt was stone . . . cold, damp limestone. What we were sitting on had been woven from the stuff of imagination . . . It was an illusion.

"Once you know what you're looking for," he said, "you'll find that a *lot* of what you see around you is that kind of magic—shallow, insubstantial—like a dream." And I knew what he meant, because I had seen how Dad's special effects worked and how a bit of latex, a bit of Karo syrup, and a lot of slick editing could be metamorphosed into celluloid reality. "And now," he said, "for your first exercise of the day . . ."

He led me through about an hour of breathing, of focusing on little black dots, of feeling my own blood racing through my veins . . . the kind of stuff they teach you in those New Age support groups in Santa Monica. I had to admit I was impatient. I wanted to *do* something, even if it was just turning the geometry teacher into a toad.

"It's no use," he said at last.

"I'm not doing it right?"

76

"Oh, you are, you are. But . . . you're not taking this seriously enough."

"Hey, dude, if you'd been inducted into 'karmic circle therapy' and 'hypno-renewal cleansing' by *your* mom at the age of thirteen, you wouldn't be able to take this stuff seriously either."

"Well, what do you want me to do?" he said, exasperated.

"Look . . . you got me into this. I never asked to have all these powers you claim I have . . . but, like, can't you just do what you're supposed to do, I mean, what it says in all those fantasy novels you can buy down at the local Book-Mart? Just teach me a few spells."

"Spells! But . . . given someone with your raw, unfocused ability . . . a spell that hasn't been thought through, been mastered with the right amount of intellectual and spiritual discipline . . . It could be very, very dangerous!"

I looked up at Anaxagoras (we were now both sitting, in lotus position, on a straw mat on the cavern floor) and he was trying very hard to look stern, but the feeling I got from him was quite different. It was, like, yielding to the inevitable . . . almost a kind of relief. Sighing, he got up, went to the stream, and pulled a big fat leather tome out of the water. It was totally dry.

"That's not really water, is it?" I said, realizing it for the first time.

"Yes . . . it's part of the illusion. But there *is* a real river running through here too . . . It is a tributary of the stream that runs into the mighty river that circumnavigates the cosmos."

"Right," I said. He opened the book, and for the first time I began to feel excited. On page after page, in twisted characters that danced up and down and sometimes actually leaped up off the parchment to flutter through the air, with illustrations that moved and sent out puffs of neon-colored smoke, with tinkling, bubbling, swooshing, clanging sound effects, there were the recipes for magic spells. This is the kind of wizardry you read about in books and see in movies . . . yeah. More like the real thing.

The titles of the spells were written in flowing Old English script. Yes! There was one that said:

Turne Ye Geometrie Teacher into a Toade (or other amphibian)

[For other amphibian, see appendix B, subsection B, sub-subsection b, sub-sub-sub-subsection b]

and I realized that the book wasn't set in stone, if you see what I mean . . . It was more like a window into an infinite book of spells, and it could pluck the spells you were looking for out of your mind and display them on the page, kind of like a big old Hypercard stack on the old school 'puter.

"Now," said Anaxagoras, "you're going to have to be very, very careful . . ." and I'm all, "Yeah, yeah," trying to read the turning-into-a-toad page, but he was too quick for me and turned to the next page, but that was just as exciting because it read:

Enchant Vehicle

turn ordinary mode of transportation into magical mode

(duration: fifteen minutes)

and I knew that *that* was something that would impress the living hell out of everyone, especially Penelope Karpovsky, and I realized that, while I had been sitting here in wizard school for like two hours, she was still there in the corridor, time-frozen in front of her locker.

"Teach me that one," I said.

"Very well," said Anaxagoras. "Repeat after me: *Thredno bizaron thaumasiastes. . . .*"

I said it over and over again until I had it memorized. And then he said, "Now, when that's all done, remember to say *'Thring!'* very clearly. That's like pushing ENTER on a computer . . . It actually *executes* the spell. It's sort of a safety device. Checks and balances, that sort of thing."

"Thanks!" I said.

"Well, I'd say you've probably had about enough for one day. Time for geometry."

I felt the familiar blurring all around me. I knew I was about to be hurled back into the emotional jungle that was Claudette Colbert High.

"Wait!" I said. "Tell me what the mirror does!"

"It sees through your eyes," said the wizard, and vanished.

11

An Enchanted Porsche

As Anaxagoras foretold, I popped back into the corridor a split second after I vanished—literally in the blink of an eye—and Penelope didn't even notice that I'd winked in and out of reality. In fact, she was in the middle of the same sentence she'd started when I disappeared; she's all, "Now, that wasn't very nice, snatching it out of my hand like that; I *was* just giving it back, you know."

And she was gazing wistfully at the mirror in my hand.

"I'm sorry, Penelope, it's just that—" How could I explain all the things that had been happening to me, and not have her laugh in my face? She touched my hand and gently turned the mirror so that she could stare into it once again. I let her do it because now I understood why she was so fascinated by what it showed her. The mirror showed what she looked like in my eyes . . . and in my eyes Penelope Karpovsky was a total goddess.

"When I look at this," she said, "sometimes I almost believe that there *is* magic. Sometimes I can almost buy that you've gone to other worlds and seen fantastic sights that other people can only see in dreams. Oh, God, I look beautiful in that mirror, more beautiful than I deserve to look."

"C'mon, Penelope," I said. "You can't say you don't deserve to be beautiful."

"But I don't," she said. "Sometimes I don't know how you can even like me."

She did have a bad case of low self-esteem. I wanted so much to comfort her, to tell her that it didn't matter to me that her family was all broken up, or why she had to spend time in family counseling. I guess what attracted me to her the most was not only that she was beautiful but she had like, this grief inside her, this pain that maybe would make most girls resentful and bad tempered, but it made her like, more sensitive. Of course I didn't think all this through right at that moment. I was standing there and she was all smiling and almost crying too, and I was all bursting with my adolescent hormones and my confusion, and I didn't think about it too hard but I kind of grabbed her by the shoulders and I kind of kissed her, except that, with the hard, cold mirror between us, it was kind of awkward, and I had to adjust my arms a couple times to keep the mirror from slipping and smashing on the linoleum between our feet.

She kind of kissed me back too, and it was cool.

In fact, things were going pretty well, weren't they? I mean, I had the fantasy car of my dreams, the girl of my dreams, *and* I had a real wizard for a guru . . . life in Encino couldn't get much better than that. I had about ten seconds of this big, old soaring feeling . . . and then I came thudding back to earth.

Buffy Margarita and Amanda Hathaway.

And Buffy's brother, Amanda's current boyfriend, a Schwarzenegger look-alike named Biff.

The three of them are all leaning against the lockers and laughing their heads off. "He kisses like a frog," Amanda says. "Eww."

Startled, I step back just a half step and that's when the mirror comes slithering out from between us like it's got a mind of its own. And before I can grab it, Biff's got the neon pink handle firmly in his fist. "Macho man," says Biff, "with your little pink hand mirror . . . ," and then he looks into it. I wonder what he sees because the next minute he's all, "Hey, look at this! How does it do this? I'm a monster!"

That's right. He's seeing himself through my vision of him, and it's not a flattering one. But I guess he's too dumb to notice, because he's all, "Hey, look, dudes, I'm a monster . . . fresh, dude!" And he's all laughing and I realize he's the kind of person who likes to be an ogre . . . being a monster feeds his ego somehow.

"Give it back," I say.

"No, come on, wait a minute," he says. And he pulls the mirror out of my reach. "Hey, Buffy, get a load of this!" He shows the mirror to her and I know what she sees because I know what my image of Buffy is like . . . a quivering, Jell-O-like, lard-laden geek . . . and I know she's not going to like this image and it's cruel of me to think this way about her but I can't help myself . . . and when she sees the image of herself, she lets out a bloodcurdling shriek and begins sprinting down the corridor. "Come back, Buffy!" Biff yells, and takes off after her and Penelope and I start running too, because she's still got the mirror in her hand.

Meanwhile, Amanda Hathaway is running along beside us and wringing her hands and she's all, "Oh, Biff, oh, Biff," all the time, and when she catches a glimpse of herself in the mirror it actually makes her hair stand on end . . . about half a can of hairspray's worth.

"Gimme that!" I try to catch up with Biff, but he tosses the mirror to Amanda. Penelope tackles Amanda and the mirror flies into the air and sprouts like, these big blue butterfly wings, and it flutters around and around Biff's head as he tries to swat it. Buffy manages to snatch it and she's all, "I'm gonna smash this thing before anyone else gets a look at it," but Biff's all, "No, don't smash it, it's fresh," and he seizes the mirror and runs all the way down the corridor, out the front entrance of the school, down the steps. . . .

For a moment I'm just standing there with my jaw dropping. Then, all at once, it hits me: That mirror is a piece of *me* . . . It sees with my eyes . . . It's a direct conduit from the outside world into the depths of my soul. It's more than just some parlor trick . . . It's my *soul* they're tossing back and forth like a basketball. I have to get it back. That's when I start running. And Penelope, racing after me, is screaming, "Aaron, Aaron, it's only a mirror—" and I know how I must look to her, my face maddened by rage.

This is when it all starts to get out of control. Buffy, Biff, and Amanda go dashing across the front lawn and into the student parking lot. I chase them. Biff leaps into a Mustang convertible and the two girls hop in after him. Without thinking, I climb into the Porsche. Penelope, beside me, is all, "Wait a minute—but you don't have your license yet and— oh, my God, did you steal this car?—"

"No, no, the producer—the plumbing—"

She gets in beside me and I start up. But Biff has already gone whizzing off down the hill in the general direction of Beverly Hills. Biff's a totally dangerous driver, and I'm all gasping at the way he's taking those curves, and I know I can't keep up . . . And Buffy's all sticking the mirror out of the window and waving it at me and reflecting off the sunlight and blinding me.

We're on Mulholland Drive now. It's a roller coaster of a street, twisting and swerving and snaking along the top of the Santa Monica Mountains. The view would be incredible if I only had time to take it in . . . the valley stretching and stretching to my left, and to the right the phantasmagorical towers of Los Angeles . . . the sun's all beating down and the wind in my face is dusty. Biff makes a sharp turn down Beverly Glen and we go bounding downhill. I have to admit that I'm getting really scared. I know something terrible's going to happen to me if I don't get the mirror back, and I know I'm doing about six illegal and unsafe things right now, not to mention risking Penelope's life . . . And *that's* when I hear the sirens and see the police lights flashing in the rearview mirror . . . And that's when I remember the *Enchant Vehicle* spell from the wizard's book of spells . . . And that's when I start to chant the words with all the fervor I can muster . . . And that's when Buffy hurls the mirror out of the window of the Mustang onto some million-dollar front porch . . . And then, at the sound of the "Thring!" . . . *That's* when the spell kicks in, and the Porsche takes off like a helicopter and . . .

"Like, oh my God," says Penelope, and I think maybe she's about to faint.

"Do you believe in magic now?"

"Yes . . . yes. . . ."

Okay, so we arc straight up against the sun. We look down and we see the policeman pulling Biff over, and we see Buffy standing by the side of the road, frantically pointing to the sky. For a moment the feeling's just awesome, because we're riding way up above the smog now . . . You can see the smog, many-clawed, wrapping itself around the city like a purple-brown crab-monster . . . and through the smog, the Capitol Needle poking up . . . You can see mountains and boulevards and shopping malls and . . . *way* to the east, Universal, perched on a bend of the mountain, with the smoke rising from the "Miami Vice" exhibit and tendriling up past the smog . . . That smog, I'm thinking to myself. Why doesn't anyone do anything about the smog?

"This is great!" says Penelope. "I think this would be a

great moment to finish what we were doing, before, you know. . . ."

And she kisses me.

I'm deliriously happy for about sixty seconds, and that's when I realize I have no idea how to make the spell stop working, and even if I did, wouldn't we come crashing down into the middle of Coldwater Canyon? I try to concentrate. I try to reach out with my mind . . . try to become one with the Porsche's inner workings. Maybe if I recite the spell backward . . . but then again, there's something elusive about the words of the spell, they seem to twist and re-form while they're streaming from my lips . . . well, I don't know if I've like said the right thing or not, but I try to execute whatever it is I've said by going like, *"Thring! Thring! Thring!"*

Bad move.

Okay, so my senses detach themselves from my body, and I feel myself start to penetrate the car's insides, but I don't touch metal, I don't feel spark plugs or hoses or gasoline . . . The substance of the car is shifting . . . It's not a car anymore, it's part flesh, part inanimate substance . . . and it's in pain . . . It's a thing that has no name, a *wrong* thing, and I know that I've created it because I've somehow overdone that magic spell, it's gone too far and it's more than just an illusion . . . It's transmuted the fabric of the car into some obscene, half-living thing.

My mind recoils in shock and that's when the Porsche really starts to go wild . . . bucking, heaving, spinning through the air . . . sprouting black leathery wings and trying to beat them against the wind . . . and Penelope's all, "Do something . . . don't you know how to drive this thing?"

But I'm just in a state of shock. Dimly I realize that we're plummeting. The car's like a newborn child, screaming, uncomprehending, all full of emotions it has no names for. I struggle to steady us. A little creative thinking—*wish* something into being, I tell myself, and at last I manage to squeeze

a parachute out of the empty air around us, and now the car's dangling from it and swaying back and forth like a Ferris wheel basket . . . and we're still falling, but slowly enough to breathe, almost. Down below us is a sea of suburbia . . . Swimming pools glitter like polished aquamarines against the steel and stucco and gold-green of citrus orchards . . . Penelope's clinging to me and I can feel her trembling . . . "We're going to hit!" she says, very softly.

"Oh, what have I done?" I said. "I'm not even supposed to be driving—and I panicked and misused the magic—and now we're—we're—" I didn't want to think about it, but at that moment I was absolutely certain we were both going to be smashed to smithereens on the pavement. I concentrated harder . . . All I had to work with was the roaring wind, but maybe if I gathered enough of it up I could . . . yes . . . all of a sudden the rescue devices started popping into being all around us . . . hot-air balloons . . . way up in the clouds, a zeppelin that was attaching itself to my steering wheel with a self-knotting rope . . . more parachutes now, pushing their way out of the exhaust pipe, thrusting up from under the seat . . . We were heading straight for some rich dude's Olympic-size swimming pool . . . we were going to crash . . . I couldn't hold all this magic anymore, couldn't keep what I was doing straight in my head . . . I was going to have to let go. . . .

We hit the water. Not too hard. I couldn't hold on to my magicking, and the car, the parachutes, the hot-air balloon, the zeppelin, all blurred and shimmered and dissipated into the summer air . . . and Penelope and I were bobbing up and down in eight feet of chlorinated water.

Penelope gasped for air. "This is pretty exciting," she said.

I couldn't see the Porsche anywhere. I guess the power of my magic had somehow totally consumed it. Maybe it was never there to begin with . . . There *was* something fishy about the way the producer had granted my wish . . . a fairy-tale air about it all that made me think that I had never quite made contact with the real world since my encounter with the dragon of the sewers. You know, like in those horror movies where the character wakes up from a nightmare only he's just inside another dream inside another dream?

We swam to the deck. This place was a total mansion. There was a commanding view of the Valley from the deck, which was all black marble with like, Greek columns and stuff and statues of nude dudes and ladies all standing around with their arms raised up in weird gestures. There was a row of tall oleander bushes that hid the rest of the lot, and from behind them came a whooshing sound . . . and when we went past the bushes we saw what it was. Beneath us, nestled in the side of the mountain, was an old-fashioned wooden roller coaster.

"Oh my God," said Penelope. "This isn't—it couldn't be—"

"Only one person around here has a roller coaster in his backyard," I said. "I read about it in *People* magazine."

We were just looking at each other in amazement when the owner of the house came wandering around the corner. "Awesome," said Tygh Simpson, the lead singer of the Senseless Vultures. "Extraterrestrial visitors. What happened to the UFO you came down on?"

"Tygh," I said, "it's me, Aaron . . . I'm Beau Maguire's kid . . . you know, the effects guy?"

"Far out," he said. "You guys want breakfast?"

"Well, like, we really need to get back to school." Penelope said.

"And we've got to find this mirror we dropped." I was more concerned about that than anything else. The last I'd seen of it, it was making a dramatic crash landing on a front porch somewhere along Coldwater Canyon.

"Look, there's probably a billion mirrors in this house, dudes," said Tygh. "I mean like, they call me a narcissist, you know? It says so right on the cover of the latest *Rolling Stone*. I wouldn't miss a mirror; help yourself."

"I don't want to seem ungrateful, Tygh, but it's like, one *particular* mirror, you know? Sentimental value."

"But you haven't seen my mirror collection yet. It's not every day that you get admitted to the greatest treasure chamber in the universe, and you're allowed to pick out one item—any item—for yourself."

"But, Tygh—"

"Aw, be casual. It's not every day Hollywood's most famous plumber drops down on me out of the sky. And anyway, I'll drive you to school afterward. In," he added, as Penelope's jaw dropped all the way to the marble paving of Tygh's patio, "my Rolls."

In a few moments we're standing inside Tygh Simpson's fabled holy of holies—his hall of mirrors. It's impossible to tell how big the room is because every inch of it is covered with a mirror surface—the walls, the ceiling—there are no windows. There is a mirror subfloor, and, a foot or so above it, the floor we're walking on is made of Plexiglas, I guess so that our feet won't soil the reflective surfaces below us. And then there are shelves and shelves—all made of mirror glass, naturally—and on the shelves are thousands upon thousands of mirrors. Little hand mirrors, full-length mirrors, mirrors with frames of tortoiseshell, neon, gold, porcelain, rattan, and good old plastic. Mirrors with ivory handles and mirrors with brass feet. Square mirrors, hexagonal mirrors, and a mirror in the shape of the Empire State Building. There were thousands of little Penelope Karpovskys and thousands of little Aaron Maguires, and even more little Tygh Simpsons, because at the very center of the hall there stood a life-size wax model of the singer.

"I know," said Tygh, "I suppose it *is* a little vain, but Madame Tussaud's, in London, they put me in their twentieth-century hall of fame, you know? And they had an extra cast of me left over. Actually, I think it looks better than the real thing. It's, you know, a virgin. And it never went through adolescence. And it's never had those long blue bouts of depression like I have."

"Yeah," Penelope said, "but if you hadn't had those bouts, we wouldn't have had songs like 'Not Human Hearts in Aspic.'"

"Yeah," Tygh said, and he sighed. "Anyway, like, help yourself; any mirror you want. On the house."

I was really worried now, because I didn't know how I could get out of it gracefully. I mean, the real mirror was lying on some porch and the longer it lay there the more nervous I was getting. I started to say something to Penelope when she cried out, "That one! That's just the thing."

She pointed all the way across the room. Talk about eyes like a hawk! There it was, sitting on a mountain of mirrors, a glint of neon pink. . . .

"How the—" I said.

Penelope started laughing. "It must have some kind of homing device," she said, and she strode over to the pile, took it, and began gazing into it once more. "It's the one, all right," she said.

"Funny," Tygh said, "I don't recognize that mirror, and I thought I knew every mirror in the house."

The most astounding thing about all this was, we were only about ten minutes late for the geometry class. When we arrived, everyone was all tittering and making suggestive comments, especially since they had all gathered by the window to see the Rolls pull in, but the teacher, whose last assignment must have been as a concentration camp guard, soon made everyone get back to work.

We decided to go home using more conventional transportation . . . skateboarding. "Who's ever going to believe it?" Penelope was saying as we reached the bottom of the hill. "A magic mirror . . . a car that flew through the air, crash-landed in a rock star's swimming pool, and vanished? Well, at least I got Tygh's autograph. But that won't prove anything."

I said, "At least *you* know now that it's true."

"Yes. I believe you now."

I was glad about that, but I couldn't really get back to the happy mood I'd been in that morning. I'd certainly learned my lesson about driving without a license . . . and as for the Porsche, easy come, easy go. I had never really deserved a reward like that anyway. The thing that haunted me was the car itself . . . the way I had awakened it to a kind of half-life. I knew I'd done something very wrong. There's a reason why metal is metal and flesh is flesh. The universe is delicately balanced, and every time I did my magic I seemed to throw that balance radically out of whack . . . It scared me.

Because I'd overused my magical energy, I'd tortured steel and rubber into consciousness. And I'd sent my mind into it and I'd felt its confusion, its anger, and its pain. And then, letting go of all that, repelled by the monster I'd created, I had crushed its being and sent it careening off into some no-man's-universe . . . some twilight zone. I had brought a kind of life into being . . . then murdered it.

And that, to me, was the scariest thing of all.

12

An Endless Ocean

The next few days were a whole lot calmer. In the mornings I worked on my geometry. Then, sometime after class, usually on my way down the corridor toward the front entrance of the school, I'd slip sidewise through the three-dimensional universe and end up in the wizard's lair. I learned to do it by myself, without being pulled in. It was easy after a while. Anyone could have done it.

The secret of traveling through different worlds and spaces is visualizing, you see. If you can really see it, you can really go there. It's not enough to see a vague image shimmering in your mind, though. You have to see, feel, touch, so firmly and so accurately that reality shifts to accommodate what you're seeing.

In my lessons I was starting to become more confident. But I didn't dare do anything as rash as I'd done with the

Porsche. If you can't control magic, if you just lash out with your mind, it ends up controlling you.

Afternoons were awesome; I'd hang out at the mall with my skater friends, Andy and Randy. Evenings Penelope would come over and we'd go to maybe Café 50s, or Johnny Rockets, or a movie. My friends were cool, and it felt good to be with Penelope, but now, more and more, there were times when I started feeling that there was something bigger than all this . . . that I was destined to be part of some awesome mega-drama that was going to be played out, you know, good and evil and all that, like in one of those myths they keep telling us about in social studies.

Don't get me wrong. I liked Penelope a lot. But there were times, sitting at Ciao Livio staring into each other's eyes over a shared cone of chocolate death ice cream, or holding hands in the middle of the latest movie with a Roman numeral in its title, that my mind would start to wander back to the wizard's cave.

I'd almost feel reality shifting right then and there, and I knew that I could, if I really willed it, step right down the aisle, past the carpet sticky with popcorn and old Coke, out the exit and right into the lair of magic. I knew I could go there without Anaxagoras even being present, because the place was as much a part of my world now as it was of his.

Anaxagoras warned me about these feelings.

"Magic," he told me, "is as seductive . . . *more* seductive than a beautiful woman. You're in love now . . . Don't deny it, a young man in love always carries a kind of pinkish aura around him wherever he goes . . . but even love doesn't seem to be able to compete with the dark allure of sorcery . . . isn't that so, Aaron?"

"I guess."

"Well . . . sorcery's just like any other thing you can become obsessed with. You can be into role-playing games . . . or be a computer nerd or a sports fanatic . . . but every now

and then you have to come up for air . . . you have to get a
life, if you know what I mean. So I'm telling you . . . take the
week off."

"But . . . you were just about to teach me about the summoning of the four winds . . . and about the transmutation of
elements . . . and about—"

"All in good time," he said. "Remember, when you're
here, time doesn't pass in the outside world, and you don't
age; so next time you come, you could even study for a week
or so . . . you know . . . camp out here, sleep over . . . we'll
even go outside the cave."

"But I thought that outside the cave was the real world."

"That's *one* outside of the cave. *Inside,* there's another
outside." Well, like, that was totally confusing, but I remembered that earlier today the geometry teacher had taught us
how to make a Möbius strip, and that was the same thing . . .
an object whose outside is its inside . . . it didn't make sense
in the real world and it didn't make sense here, but I knew
that it was true.

"All right," Anaxagoras said finally. "Enough of that, and
let's get back to your visualization exercises." Which was fun
in a New Age sort of way.

I closed my eyes. I sent my mind out and let it skim the
surface of the marble . . . let it run along the pages of the
wizard's leather-bound book of spells . . . I could feel the life
in the leather . . . In the leather, there still danced the anguish
of a dying animal . . . In the parchment, the ink spots
whirled . . . I sent my mind along the stream that flowed
through the cave . . . It seemed like a little brook when I
touched its surface, but when I dived underneath the surging
current I could feel another, swifter river beneath, and beneath that another, and another, and another . . . and then it
seemed that I touched an ocean much bigger than any ocean
in the world, and it was an ocean that was totally still, and
quiet, so that I could like hear myself think for the first time

in my life. And that was weird, hearing my thoughts . . . well, seeing them almost . . . each thought a neon-colored flare, flickering and darting away like those deep-sea fish, you know, the ones that glow in the dark . . . I saw a lot of stuff that I thought I'd forgotten. I remembered being a baby. I remembered a time when our house wasn't divided in two. I remembered that my parents had once been in love. Now, that was an alien concept, and the memory wasn't all rosy . . . it was full of pain too. And I got the feeling that grief and joy were two sides of the same thing; and other so-called opposites too, like man and woman, like reality and illusion. It was pretty cosmic, I guess, and I stayed there, in the ocean, drinking in the water and seeming to grow wiser with each drop. That was when I realized that I wanted my parents to get back together again. And that was something magic couldn't do.

Then, from like infinitely far away, I heard the wizard's voice: "Tell me what you see, Aaron."

"An ocean," I said.

"What is the ocean called?" he asked me.

"Love," I said, knowing it for the first time.

"Come back now. Ease your way slowly back. Don't hurry. It's like deep-sea diving. It can be fatal to pull out of the Endless Ocean too fast. Easy now. Easy."

I blinked and I was back in the cave.

And there was something else in the cave with us. It was the producer's Porsche, unscathed and unscratched, washed and waxed and parked between two large stalagmites. "Now, what," said the wizard, "are you going to do with this car?"

"Oh . . . *thanks,*" I said, because I'd been dreading the day when Dad's producer would suddenly ask him how I was doing with the gift he'd sent me. Then I thought about how badly I'd treated the car . . . driving without a permit and flying it and crashing it into Tygh Simpson's swimming pool . . . and I said, "I guess I should really say to him, 'I'm really grateful, but I don't think I'm ready to own something like that. . . .' "

"It's your decision," said the wizard. "But I'm glad you're a tad more mature now than when we first met. Well, you'd better hurry up and do whatever you have to do. . . ."

And I knew why too. I'd flicked the car with the edge of my mind. It was an illusion car. The real car was gone forever, and magic couldn't make it come back. This car might act and look perfectly real for a long time, or it might not . . . but at some stage it was going to deteriorate into smoke . . . like the phantom that it was.

"All right now," said the wizard. "Do your exercises, and we'll meet again next week."

"But what if I—"

"Well," said the wizard, "if you have an unbearable urge to make magic, you can work on the mirror some more."

And all of a sudden I was back in the driveway of my house, and the Porsche was parked right there; it was a little shinier, a little brighter than a real car would have been . . . just like a special effects shot in a movie has to be more vivid than the real thing, just to convince people that it's real.

The messages on my machine were the same old thing: Dad's divorce lawyer, Mom's divorce lawyer, both of them wanting to have a meeting with me and trying to bribe me with dinner at the Hard Rock Café. Message from Mom, saying she'd be on the next plane out, as soon as she finished inspecting the warehouse in Katmandu. Dad wouldn't be home for dinner; the exploding kangaroo had to be reshot after the gore police at the studio had a cow. Well, luckily, I was supposed to meet Penelope that afternoon, and I got out my skateboard and jammed on down to the mall. I had the mirror in my back pocket, of course; I hadn't let it out of my possession since the day Biff and Buffy ran off with it. But I still didn't really have the courage to look into it that closely.

I guess I was afraid of what I might see . . . of what my true self-image might be.

I didn't know when Penelope was going to show up exactly—she had one of those family turmoil support group things today—so I just cruised around for a while. I wasn't looking forward to a week without magic. Maybe I'd gotten a little bit addicted to it; maybe it was right for the wizard to make me take a break, get a little distance from it all. But I wasn't convinced. I wanted to know more. I mean, he'd told me often enough that I had more talent than he did at my age, that I was like, a natural. Why couldn't he teach me everything *now*? Hey, maybe he was jealous.

That was a cool theory. I had fantasies of me outstripping the wizard, the tables being turned, of me stalking around in flowing robes and Anaxagoras mopping the floor of the cave, like Mickey Mouse in that Disney movie.

I ended up at the arcade, where I spent six or seven quarters on the new Galactic Kung Fu Masters game. I heard a familiar laugh. I looked up and I could see the back of Penelope's head. She was giggling. I wasn't too pleased when I realized that she was talking to Buffy and Amanda. Suddenly I thought I heard my name. I decided to stay there, crouched behind the video game, and listen to what they were saying.

13

Temptation

Penelope's all telling them about what it's like to fly. She's all, "It's better than a video game. It's better than riding an airplane or zooming down Psychlone at Magic Mountain. It's even better than that new virtual reality show they've got down in the convention center, the one where Timothy Leary lectures you and you get to try out the gloves and the helmet. . . ."

Amanda's all, "Oh, Penelope, you're so full of it. What's happened to you anyway? Since you started going out with Aaron, you've like, turned into such a dweeb. You start spouting sci-fi fantasies at a moment's notice, and you get all weird and dreamy, and we're all 'Earth to Penelope, Earth to Penelope,' but it doesn't make any difference."

"Yeah, dudette," says Buffy, "you've never levitated, so stop going on and on about it like you're some kind of authority."

"Well—" says Penelope, "but you saw it! I mean, when you guys stole the mirror and we started chasing you across Mulholland Drive—we took to the air in our Nine-Eleven and—"

"Give me a break!" says Amanda. "Aaron with a Porsche? That geek?"

"He's no geek," says Buffy. "Well, at least he's a skater. But no way does he have a Porsche."

Penelope's about as frustrated as she can be. She's standing there stamping her foot and clenching her fists and, I admit, looking totally fetching. She knows they witnessed this display of magic, but I know something that she doesn't know—that magic happens under people's noses all the time, but it takes a special kind of talent to notice. Because you have to see past the illusions that are continually generated by the eternal interplay of smoke and mirrors. This is something I learned in those long sessions of concentration, of gathering my mind, of visualizing. In fact, if Penelope wasn't a special kind of girl, she might not have known she was whizzing through the air at all . . . She might have experienced something a lot more down-to-earth . . . like a quick walk around the school grounds.

Okay, I'm all listening to the girls talking about yours truly, and meanwhile, around me, the video games are thrumming, chirping, tweeting, clanking, and whooshing. I'm so intent on listening to the girls that it takes me a moment to notice that there's a chubby hand on the joystick in front of me, and a row of grubby quarters lined up beneath the monitor.

"Come on, dude," says some little kid, "you lost your 'continue.' Let me play now, okay?"

"Uh, yeah."

"Aaron Maguire is not an ordinary human being," Penelope Karpovsky says in hushed, reverential tones. I'm blushing.

"He's a sorcerer's apprentice—he met this guy—this *wizard,* as in, you know, Merlin—and he's taking lessons from him."

"What are you talking about?" says Buffy. "So what? I met Arnold Schwarzenegger once. That doesn't make me the world's biggest muscleman."

"No, no, no . . . you just don't understand . . . I'm talking wizardry . . . clouds of smoke, making Porsches fly, turning people into frogs. . . ."

Amanda's all, "Here he comes!" because right then is when I slip into view. I always seem to be sneaking up on them. They look at each other, kind of guiltily.

Penelope's all, "Aaron. Did I tell them too much?"

I had a feeling that being a student of wizardry wasn't something that was supposed to get widely known around the school, but there was no way for me to deny it, or agree with it, without getting deeper into it. So I just stood there looking all goofy and sort of trying to signal to Penelope that maybe we should go somewhere and leave the others behind.

"Hey, Aaron!" said Amanda. "Turn Mrs. Ogilvy into a frog."

"Yeah," said Buffy. "Maybe she'll have a better chance of getting kissed."

"Aaron is *too* a wizard," said Penelope, furiously, and before I could stop her she's all, "and he's going to prove it to you right now."

"Yeah, right," said her companions in chorus.

"You won't laugh when you see what Aaron can do . . . I bet he'll summon up a dragon or something just like that, and we can scare all the mall rats. You know like it'll be like Godzilla stomping on Tokyo or something and it'll make a real big scene here with choppers and sirens and news anchors and . . . and get on the evening news so our parents will, like, *finally* pay attention to us for once."

"Penelope, you know I can't do that. . . ."

"Yes, you can," she said. "I know you can. And you will.

101

You *will*. You will, won't you, Aaron?" and she's all squeezing my shoulder and causing my hormones to go ballistic.

"Sure I can, er, will," I said, which was far from certain. What was I going to do about it? I tried calling Anaxagoras . . . reaching out with my mind and sending out help signals through the mystical ether. No luck, though. I couldn't feel his presence anywhere. Stood to reason he'd be able to mask his vibes from me; I'd do the same thing myself if I were a wizard in a world of wizards.

I became conscious of the three girls staring weirdly at me. I realized that I must have been zoning out and that I must look like some kind of psycho, all standing there with my mind stretched halfway across the world and only tenuously connected to my body.

But Penelope's all, "Be quiet and wait. You'll see. And then you'll believe me. This is totally going to be great."

Where are you, Anaxagoras? I call out with my mind. *I really need you . . . I just don't know what to do . . . I feel I'm being bulldozed into doing something I know isn't right, and yet I can't seem to stop myself. . . .*

There's nothing. It's like my voice is totally echoing around me, like I'm standing in a dark, deep cavern that doesn't end . . . and then finally, at the very end of the echoing, when my voice has died to nothing, I seem to hear a still small voice reply: *You're on your own, kid. Gone fishing.*

Well, if my guru and grand master wasn't even going to give me advice, what was I going to do? I said to the girls, "Right. You asked for fireworks, and you're going to get them. But don't say I didn't warn you." I said it in this fierce, awesome voice, and the three girls shrank back against the side of a big old Neo-Geo game. Suddenly I felt powerful, like Dr. Frankenstein must have felt just before he threw that switch.

Smoke was pouring out of my ears. Red smoke, green smoke, purple smoke, yellow smoke. This was a cheap trick, just an illusion really, but the girls started to scream, and then some of the other kids in the arcade noticed it too because, although I'd focused the illusion on the three girls, illusions have a habit of leaking out into the real world.

Summoning a dragon, I thought. How hard could it be? Maybe just an image of a dragon superimposed over the tile-and-marble decor of the mall. If only I could lay my hands on the wizard's spell book. . . .

I pulled the smoke into tendrils, spun the tendrils into whorls, boomeranged the whorls across the arcade while the girls were all, "Oh my God," and "Eww," and "Kewl," and "Fresh," and all the things they like to say, except for Penelope, who just stood there silently, smiling a little at the dancing smoke . . . wistful, a little sad. I remembered why she said she wanted me to work a mighty spell: ". . . so our parents can, like, *finally* notice us." I still hadn't met her parents, only heard her talk endlessly about therapy and encounter sessions and support groups and family counseling, and I couldn't help wondering about what life was really like for her. I mean, sure, me and half my friends think of our families as dysfunctional, but . . . we don't go around encased in a bubble of sadness even when we are having a good time. I was tempted to stop the magic show and to send my mind probing into hers, and I knew that I had the power to do that, but I got the feeling she wasn't ready to open up that much, and I didn't want to be all spying on her dark secrets.

So there I was, the eye of a minihurricane, enjoying the way those girls were all gasping and shrieking. I concentrated hard on the spell book. I could see the spell book now, caught up in the wind between universes, the pages fluttering, the characters dancing. *I want to know more,* I told myself. I sent my mind soaring now, cracking the wall between worlds to the secret place, outside space and time, where the cave of magic lay—

And then, all at once, I was there. The book was in my arms, and it weighed more than it ought to weigh . . . as if it carried in its pages all the pain and all the illusion in the world. Around me, the limestone caverns were forming and unforming . . . I was sort of dissolving in and out between the two worlds . . . Now I could see the video arcade and now I couldn't . . . The pages were flying now, some of them actually ripping free and flapping against my face . . . letters glowed and glittered and danced . . . illustrations scrolled across the parchment and melted into thin air. . . .

"Dragons!" I shouted. A vellum sheet peeled away from the book and wrapped itself around my face. The book was too heavy to hold. I stepped in something wet and I suddenly realized that the river—the little stream that stretched all the way down to the great Ocean of Love that surrounds the cosmos—that stream was overflowing its banks, and it was going to drown me if I didn't get out of there fast. And the book of spells was going to drag me under—the water was raging now. It was a rainbow-colored, sparking water, some-times like fire, sometimes like smoke. I let go of the book. Only the single page remained, plastered to my cheeks, as the tide carried me up and sent me flying up, up, up, like I was surfing, I guess, and shooting through some tubular tunnel of darkness where at the other end I could still see the three girls, peering at me in awe and wonderment.

So, like, there I was as the smoke subsided, standing in a video arcade in a shopping mall, feeling like a doofus.

"Cool," said Amanda Hathaway, "but where's the dragon?"

"There won't be any dragon," I said. "No more tricks today. I'm tired now. You've all had enough."

It was then that I looked down at the piece of paper I was holding. In glowing, Old English letters, the title read:

FOR THE SUMMONYNGE OF DRAGONS

kids: don't try this at home

and I realized that I was doomed to see this thing through to the end, because when I agreed to summon the dragon, I had already unleashed the chain of events that would lead to the summoning.

As Anaxagoras told me during our lessons, the words of a wizard are not like ordinary words—they're not just air and carcinogens. A wizard's words—even spoken in jest—are echoes of the great truths that brought the world into being. Magic consists of knowing the true names of things, and the right words to say. When you say the wrong words, you set things in motion that have a life of their own.

That is, you see, one of the greatest perils of wizardry, as I was about to discover.

14

Unchaining the Dragon

The spell seemed pretty simple. There were only three magic words in it. I can't repeat them here or everyone'll start doing it, and dragons'll be as common as cockroaches, and as boring. Yeah, the spell was simple all right, but there was a lot of fine print. This was the sort of thing it said:

> 1. *Dragon:* Before unchaining the dragon, it is important to know exactly what a dragon is. A dragon can be either substantive, metaphorical, animatronic, or high-concept. For notes on the latter, see paragraph 27 (b), subsection Q, epigram 32.

2. N.B.: The *Dragon* is, of course, your own self. No dragon can be created that does not draw on the dark essence of the sorcerer's soul. If you don't have a soul, refer to the manual. Dragons will not self-destruct unless previously programmed to do so. Remove the CPU, clap thrice, and, if you believe in fairies, see paragraph 17, verse 12.

3. No responsibility is taken for unclaimed fewmets.

4. A dragon is defined according to the principles of magic as a *concretization* of natural or unnatural forces or principles into quasi-reptilian somatic nexus and no guarantee is provided of mythological integrity, conformance to preconceived visual effect, or tameness.

5. Make sure you are in a wide, open space with little public traffic before commencing enchantment; otherwise, the terrorization factor of public opinion may ...

6. dragon dragon dragon dragon dragon

Well: The print wasn't just fine, it seemed to get finer and finer as it went along. "What are you reading?" said Penelope. "All I can see is a bunch of little squiggly markings."

I was squinting and squinting, and it seemed totally uncool to be standing there looking stupid and peering at the old parchment, so I folded it up and stuck it in my back pocket along with the magic mirror of my soul. "I'm done," I said. "I'm ready to do the big deed now, so let's get on with it." Actually the small print was swimming around in my head.

It couldn't be that important, I thought to myself. I mean, like, if it was so important they'd have printed it bigger, wouldn't they? And anyway, I knew I was a powerful wizard already ... more powerful than Anaxagoras had been at my age ... wasn't that so? I could do it. I was going to put on a display of magical pyrotechnics such as Encino had never witnessed. Yeah.

"Be very, very quiet," I said, in a passable imitation of Elmer Fudd.

I was already getting in touch with my magical abilities, because it was like the sound in the arcade was suddenly turned off. The games were all still going on, but silently, and the people were all moving in like, slow motion. It was cool. The whole world seemed to be catching its breath, waiting for me to pull the rabbit out of the hat ... and the three girls were looking at me in awe. I picked up my skateboard from where I'd leaned it against a video game, in case I needed to make a quick getaway if things got out of hand. I spread my arms wide ... noticing for the first time that I was wearing these awesome robes, embroidered with suns, moons, and stars, that billowed out on every side of me like the sails of a ship. The sleeves hung all the way to the ground and the stars, suns, and moons glittered as they revolved around one another.

So I stand there looking way cool for about ten minutes. You can cut the tension with a ginsu. At last I'm all, "Drumroll, please."

This is how the drumroll comes: First it's nothing more than a vibration ... You can hardly feel it ... It's like the pre-earthquake feeling that some people get ... And then it starts building up and building up, and soon I'm pretty sure the entire shopping mall is shaking and shaking and ... It's too late to turn back now, so quickly I say the three magic words, at the same time reaching deep inside my mind ... reaching for the dragon within ... Wasn't that what the small print said, that "no dragon can be created that does not draw on the dark essence of the sorcerer's soul?"

What *is* the dragon that draws on the dark essence of the sorcerer's soul? And suddenly I find myself racing once more down the sewer pipes of the universe. There's a shadowy *thing* that's just ahead of me, a small and slippery thing that maybe I can grasp if only I'm quick enough—

I've caught the dragon.

Who are you? I scream to the darkness inside myself. And the dragon starts to turn and I see the sewer-monster that's eluded me before, and I see that it has the face of a demon and the eyes of a teenage boy—*my eyes*—

"*Thring!*" I shout at the top of my lungs.

—and then *boom, boom, boom,* every video screen in the arcade goes *kerash!* at the same time, and there's this wind that whips up all the shards of glass and carries them up toward the ceiling where they whirl and glitter . . . but where's the dragon? I don't see any dragon anymore. "No dragon can be created that does not draw on the dark essence of the sorcerer's soul." Yeah, well, c'mon, maybe I just don't have a dark essence.

What is the part of myself I dare not face? I cast my mind back . . . to the monster in the sewer . . . and everything's spinning and . . . spinning and . . . suddenly I know that the dragon is here after all. Because I do have a dark essence. Everyone does.

Everything's still quiet in the video arcade. The girls are still standing there, watching me curiously as I zone in and out. There's no dragon, is there? Only a sense of unease. A prickling at the base of my spine, the nape of my neck. I see that Penelope's shivering.

"Wish the air conditioning wasn't set so high," Amanda says. Her eyes dart back and forth and I know it's not the air-conditioning that's got her all nervous.

Suddenly Buffy begins to scream. She points her finger

toward the doorway. She's screaming in monster-movie style, you know, the kind of screaming that makes your ears pop. We all turn to look. It's a dragon, all right.

"Hey! It's *cute!*" Penelope says.

It sure is. It's no bigger than a bullfrog. It stands in the doorway. It's garishly lit by the neon arcade sign. It's slinky and scaly and it's a dragon all right.

"I don't like it," says Buffy.

But Penelope's all, "Oh, you animal hater," and she goes right over and scoops the thing up in her hand, and it sort of yaps and runs up her shoulder, and now it's licking her earlobe. "Slimy," she says, but she's laughing.

"Eww, gross," says Amanda.

"Why don't you kiss it?" says Buffy. "Maybe it'll, like, turn into some totally handsome prince."

"You wish," Penelope says, and then, smiling shyly at me. "I already have one, thanks." The dragon leaps off her shoulder. "You know," she adds, "the dragon kind of looks like you, Aaron . . . it has your eyes."

But there's something about this dragon that still makes me nervous. It can't be the way it's running around in circles, like a dog chasing its own tail. Maybe it's the fact that it *does* have my eyes. Somehow the dragon and I are one. Because I can almost feel it breathing. I can almost hear its thoughts, thoughts I've thought myself but have never dare admitted that I thought.

Suddenly it scoots out of the video arcade and the girls and I follow it. It has a hard time with the marble-tiled floor and it's kind of slipping and sliding. A bevy of Girl Scouts comes charging through and the dragon disappears into their midst. They scream and they scatter just as though he's like, a mouse or something, and one of the security guards comes trotting up to see what's up.

"There he goes!" Amanda shouts. The dragon's skittering past the scenic elevator.

111

A woman with a baby carriage and a bird's-nest hat bolts so fast that the hat goes sailing over the balcony down toward the next level. The security guard's all scratching his head and trying to figure out what's going on, and the Girl Scouts have ganged up on him and they're all chattering in twenty dialects of Valspeak.

"I don't see him," says Penelope.

Just then, the dragon comes lumbering around the corner where there's a May Company, a Japanese gadget store, and a toy store. I say lumbering because it's not a little dragon anymore. It's about the size of a baby elephant, and it's coughing up smoke.

"Is he sick?" says Buffy.

I'm all, "No. I think . . . he's trying to breathe fire."

"Make him shrink back again," says Amanda. "He's like, more manageable when he's small."

But I didn't know how to do that, and the dragon wasn't just lumbering anymore, it was pretty much bounding, and each footfall made the whole mall shake and dented the marble, and the shoppers were panicking now.

Across the way, a movie theater's all letting out, and the dragon's stamping its feet, and the theater patrons are running, tripping over each other, screaming, and doing everything you're supposed to do in a monster movie. In fact, a couple of Asian tourists are staring, pointing, snapping pictures, and yelling *"Gojira! Gojira!"* at the top of their lungs. They probably think it's the Universal Studios tour. The dragon lets out a roar now, and it's spreading its wings, and it's getting a lot bigger now—in fact, it's banging its head against the skylight. . . .

I've got to do something. I'm the one who unchained the dragon and I guess I'm the only one who can send him back where he came from. "Quick," I shout. "The rate he's growing, he's gonna burst out of this mall like a chick through an eggshell." Penelope and I, with the other two girls jogging

112

along behind, make for the escalators. Maybe I can confront the dragon outside, where there's room to maneuver. We're racing down the escalator (it's an up escalator, but it's faster because the down escalator is crammed with panicking people), and the dragon's already smashed up the window of the video arcade and is now lashing at a clothing store with its tail . . . and getting a lot better at breathing fire. In fact, it's getting kind of hot in the mall.

My mind is racing to find a way out of this. There has to be a solution. I cry out Anaxagoras's name, but he doesn't magically appear to bail me out. I realize that he's never put any tools in my hand that he didn't expect me to figure out all by myself, and I'm thinking that even this summoning may be some kind of test, but I also have this sinking feeling, like when you know you're going to flunk a final and you think maybe your whole career may depend on it and you see your future flushing itself down the toilet. . . .

I still have the skateboard under my arm and the parchment tucked in my back pocket with the mirror. We run all the way down three flights of up escalators, and we can feel the whole shopping mall vibrate with each draconian lurch.

"What are you doing, Aaron?" Buffy screams. "Are you going to just, like, run away?"

We're doing just that. I know it's the wrong thing to do but I have to buy time. Out in the front parking lot of the Galleria, there's like a dozen news vans out already, plus there's a chopper from Fox News hovering above us. The sky is purple with smog. Several anchorpersons are already jabbering away at various cameras. People are streaming out of the mall like ants, not even bothering to look for their cars. Traffic on Ventura Boulevard has gone insane. A reporter corners me.

"Kid, what's it like in there?"

"Pretty hair-raising," I say.

"Best publicity stunt in years, isn't it?" says the reporter. "I heard the dinosaur's like forty feet long."

"It's not a dinosaur," I say, "it's a—"

"Like, oh my God," says Amanda. We all look over toward the boulevard, right by Tower Records, where an Incredibly Famous Director has just stepped out of a white stretch limousine. The reporters are swooping down like vultures, except for one of the network's women, who's still in the middle of recording her segment. . . .

"And this is Arabella Benihana speaking to you live from Encino in the San Fernando Valley, where a dinosaur has just been seen terrorizing the Galleria. It's all the brainchild of Incredibly Famous Director Max Halperin, whose ninety-million-dollar extravaganza, Cretaceous Shopping Mall, *is opening next week at seventeen thousand theaters nationwide. And here's our resident dinosaur expert, paleontologist William Warren, to tell us what kind of dinosaur we're about to see emerging from the mall. . . ."*

The Incredibly Famous Director is being mobbed, and he's loving every moment of it. The whole plaza is chock full of people now, and suddenly there's a big collective scream of terror and delight and we all turn around and see the dinosaur.

It's not my dragon at all. It's a big old latex-and-metal tyrannosaurus rex, and it's stalking up and down the parking lot, now and then pausing to kick a car out of the way.

"Those aren't real cars," Buffy says, disgusted.

"But what happened to the dragon?" Penelope says.

That's when we hear the familiar drumroll-cum-earthquake that always seems to presage the coming of disaster. The whole parking lot's rocking back and forth, but no one's running for safety . . . everything *must* be okay, after all. We're on a movie set, aren't we? And this is movieland, where nothing can hurt us. I alone seem to feel that there's something else going on. I turn away from the Animatronic dinosaur and

114

look in the other direction, at the monstrous mass of glass and concrete that is the shopping mall at the heart of our magic kingdom, and I'm the only one who sees it shatter . . . the only one who sees the dragon burst loose out of its stone imprisonment.

The dragon is a vast thing now. It straddles the whole shopping center. But the walls are knitting together and the glass is unshattering itself. The dragon is huge but it's tenuated, shadowy . . . and I see that Penelope is right . . . it has my eyes. The sky seems to be clearing and I realize the dragon is still growing . . . feeding on the smog itself . . . eating up the pollution as it pours from a million vehicles and a thousand factories into the stagnant bowl of air that is the Valley, locked in by its ring of mountains.

I turn to the three girls. "This is getting dangerous," I say. "It's not a game anymore."

Buffy says, "That was cool, Aaron! But I want to see if I can get Max's autograph." So she and Amanda race toward the growing mob that's descended on the Incredibly Famous Director in a feeding frenzy.

Only Penelope is left, and I tell her, "The dragon . . . can't you see it? . . . It's still here . . . we still have to. . . ."

And Penelope looks up at where I'm looking, and I can tell that she can't see what I'm seeing. But she takes hold of my hand, and she says to me softly, "I believe you, Aaron. I can't see what you're seeing, but I know you can see things other people can't see. I know there's magic in you. Don't worry about those girls—they're never going to understand. But I do. And I'll always believe in you."

My heart aches because she's saying things I wish my parents would say to me sometimes. And I realize there comes a moment in your life when you start to see your childhood, and being at home with your parents, and all that, as fading into the past. That's what happens when a hero fights the

115

dragon and wins the maiden, I guess . . . It's like defying your parents and leaving home.

I tell her, "Well, like, now I have to go and battle the dragon."

"Why, sure, Aaron," she says, and she kisses me.

"I'll be back," I say, but I'm not really so sure about that as I watch the dragon spread its wings and take off, south, toward the Santa Monica Mountains and the sea. Grimly I set down the skateboard on the pavement and—trying not to lose control now—I start reciting the words of the vehicle enchantment spell.

15

Smoke and Mirrors

All over Los Angeles, thousands of toilets were backing up. The smog was roiling over the city, gathering like thunderclouds in the sunset. Fumes from millions of rush-hour vehicles were spiraling skyward, then twisting around each other, weaving in and out like the threads of a monstrous carpet that would cover the city and smother it to death.

Well, that's what the news will say is happening right now, with the air quality index plummeting in a freak nosedive and the sewer system of the city clogged by an unprecedented, shapeless *thing*, reaching like a million-armed octopus down the pipes and out of the septic tanks of the city. But that's *real* reality, and here in magic reality, it's slightly different . . . Here in magic reality, it's just Aaron versus the dragon. And the dragon's turning left, heading northeast now, sucking up pollution like a sperm whale lapping up krill.

I get on my enchanted skateboard. Jagged sparks fly from the trucks and the board glows with weird solarized colors. I turn to Penelope one more time, and I say, "I'll see you later."

She says, despairing, "Where, Aaron?"

And I say, "I don't know . . . um . . . follow your heart," which is the kind of thing you hear in soap operas or something, but I can't think of anything else, and it seems to ring true for her, because she nods and she's all, "Yeah, Aaron . . . I'll find you," and she turns away from me and starts to walk across the street. Then a sudden thought strikes me and I cry after her, "Meet me where the smog ends." She seems to understand although, like, I don't, because she turns and waves to me and gives me a thumbs-up sign. There's a lump in my throat as I watch her cross and walk slowly up the hill in the direction of her house.

My skateboard's totally glowing now and I take off after the dragon. I barely skim the pavement and I leave a neon-bright afterburn trail along the concrete. On either side of me are the fashionable boutiques of Encino, streaming past in a haze of rainbow colors. I follow the dragon that snakes up Ventura Boulevard like a big old blob of darkness, sucking up the colors of the city.

The dragon's growing by the minute, pulling its energy out of the smog and the sewers. Its breath is fiery and foul. Its tail lashes against the freeway overpass, spewing black slashes over the tangled mass of taggers' signatures. It's heading skyward and I follow him. The skateboard zooms upward and does a couple of three-sixties, and I squeeze my eyes tight shut and pray that the centrifugal force will be enough to keep my sneakers stuck to the grip tape. The dragon's totally crossing over the Santa Monica Mountains now and I follow him, and the wind is screaming in my ears and like, looking down, I see the teenagers drag-racing along the twists and turns of Mulholland Drive. They don't stop to gape at me

because I'm not there for them ... The battle that will rage
between me and the dragon is a battle within.

We're streaking over Beverly Hills now—over the jigsaw
quilt of emerald lawns and turquoise swimming pools. The
dragon's breath spews over manicured gardens and fairy-tale
mansions. People are rushing out of their houses, getting out
of their Mercedeses, pointing at the sky, but I know they don't
know I'm there. With my double vision, I can see what they
see: the mud and dust exploding out of the air like fireworks—
nothing supernatural, just an environment gone mad. I try to
spur on my skateboard. I want to use the *Enchant Vehicle*
spell again, bump it up to a higher gear ... but I don't want
to go out of control like I did before.

The dragon screams as it flies up Sunset. Its great leathery wings beat the air and create great whirlwinds of foul-
smelling mud. I follow, grim faced. The dragon's tail lashes
at the gaudy dragon that's draped over the top of the Chinese
Theater. The lights of evening are starting to come on as the
sun sets ... brilliant neons ... tourists are milling about, peering at the Hollywood stars in the pavement, trying out the
celebrities' footprints in front of the Chinese Theater ... and
the boulevard's filling up with noxious fumes. There's a chorus
of coughing and spluttering, and the cloud is so thick I can
barely see the traffic as I dash through the mist above it. But
I can hear tires squealing and pileups and stuff, and more and
more I'm getting to realize just how big of a mess this is. But
it's my mess and I'm the only one who can fix it.

The dragon keeps moving and growing. It fills the whole
boulevard now. It's squishing against Frederick's and ramming
its head against the two-story McDonald's ... It's a bizarre-
looking monster, part Chinese New Year dragon, part slime
mold from hell, part animated garbage dump ... It's picking
up more and more smog, sucking it in ... attracting all the
empty cans and uncollected trash along the sidewalk until it's
studded with like this aluminum chain mail ... It's clanking

and it's roaring and I'm the only one who can see that it's a living, breathing thing, with eyes and a face that look like me on a *totally* bad Monday morning and with a dark soul smoldering with rage. I'm the only one who knows this as I race behind it on my skateboard that's accelerating now . . . overtaking the traffic . . . right on the monster's tail. We get to the Hollywood Bowl, where there's like a *humongous* traffic jam because of a Senseless Vultures concert. The dragon takes one awe-inspiring breath and this acid rain stuff just comes gushing out of the sky on top of the crowd that's crawling all over the seats trying to find some place to duck under. The dragon's tail flicks over the flashing Hollywood Bowl sign, and it goes tumbling down Highland Avenue and crashes into that big church that was in *War of the Worlds*.

The dragon's heading east, toward Griffith Park, rearing up to bite the needle off the top of the Capitol Records tower—I don't know Hollywood that well. I'm a valley dude through and through, but I can see the HOLLYWOOD sign up there on the hill. Somewhere, somehow, I'm going to have to take a stand. I'm going to have to become the mythic hero that I'm not. How can I do that? I send my thoughts out, searching for images from heroic legends . . . but I've never been good at mythology, never paid that much attention in Mrs. Bronfermakher's class . . . and so all I find are little flashes of stories that Mom used to tell me . . . in the old days . . . before my parents started fighting.

Even while I'm trying to become a hero, I find that I'm already changing. My skateboard is bucking and heaving, and all at once I'm on a white steed, caparisoned in cloth-of-gold . . . and I'm wearing, like, all this armor and stuff . . . but it's not heavy because it's woven out of memories and fantasies.

I need a weapon and I reach into the billowing smog and pull out a flaming sword . . . and my horse whinnies and rears as it charges uphill, and suddenly it has white feathery wings, and it's beating them furiously as it races the dragon.

The next thing I know, we're up there in the Hollywood Hills. The dragon is coiled around Griffith Observatory. There's supposed to be a laser show going on inside, but it can't be as exciting as what's going on here. I hold my sword aloft and I spur on the winged steed and rush straight at the dragon's jaws. It yawns wide. Its teeth are like a row of machetes. I swing the sword. It's all, *crack!* against one of the teeth, and sparks fly everywhere, and the dragon roars and I swing upward to avoid its tongue. Talk about halitosis! The air is one big case of morning breath. I raise my arms wide and cry out for something that'll quell the stench, and it starts raining mouthwash.

I fly down lower and try to fly full tilt, sword outstretched, at where the dragon's heart ought to be, but I'm only guessing . . . My sword strikes something, I don't know what. There's a wound. Something dark and mushy oozes out. It smells like an exploding septic tank.

But I can't stop to hold my breath so I hit the dragon's flanks again and again. Fire comes spurting from my sword . . . Fire runs up the triple-thick garbage and the garbage catches fire and the dragon's all rolling up and down the hillside, trying to put itself out. It keeps exhaling great gusts of muck, drenching all the cars in the observatory's parking lot with icky brown goo. It thrashes against the greenery until pretty soon part of the hillside's on fire and like, I can see someone calling 911 on his car phone, and in a minute I can hear the fire engines. I have to draw the dragon away from here or else the city will choke on its own pollution. It's attacking blindly right now, and I'm no more to it than like, a horsefly or something, in spite of my fancy Pegasus and my fiery sword.

I fly right up to its ear and I'm all screaming down there, "Leave L.A. alone, dude . . . It's *me* you should be after . . . I unchained you . . . I brought you into this reality . . . It's *me* here, Aaron Maguire . . . and I made you out of my inner darkness." Yeah. All dragons are one. All monsters come from inside ourselves. That's what the fine print had said, hadn't it? But it hadn't sunk in until now.

So the dragon hears my name . . . It echoes and reechoes as it goes down its ear . . . and it kind of totally shudders all over, almost as though it's hearing its *own* name.

It cranes its neck and looks at me with its huge, glowering eyes.

And I realize that I *have* called the dragon by its own name, because it and I are somehow linked to each other, part of each other . . . and the dragon's not an *it* anymore but a real person, someone deeply familiar to me. He glares at me, and there's a bitterness in his eyes and I hear his voice reverberating in my mind . . . *Why did you dredge me up out of the labyrinth? Don't you know it's better to let sleeping dragons lie?*

And I'm all, "If you are my inner darkness, what are you doing beating up on Los Angeles?"

And he's all, *There's enough darkness in a single human soul to destroy the whole world. And you've unchained it . . . you stupid little sorcerer's apprentice . . . and I'll keep growing and growing until I consume the universe.* And he laughs, that "muahahaha" kind of evil villain laugh that's in every mad scientist movie. And my blood runs cold.

But my steed is pawing the air and snorting lightning bolts, and my sword is still burning, and I still know that I'm the only one who can get us out of this mess. So I say, "Before you consume the universe, dude, you're going to have to consume *me* first. Because if you're the dark side of me, then I'm the light side of *you*, and you can't become totally evil unless you destroy me first."

When he hears this he's all shrieking . . . it's a blood-curdling sound . . . and he rushes at me all at once. I concentrate with all my might and I tell the steed to swerve up into the air, and now it's the dragon who's chasing me, and I'm arcing up through the turbulent smog and jamming away from the city, toward the sea.

We whiz over Hollywood and West Hollywood and do a quick spin around the Hard Rock Café, and then we career through Beverly Hills and past the Sacramento Freeway and now we're blasting our way through Venice. The beach is just ahead and the sun is big and bloated and purpled with smog. Along the beachfront, there're hundreds of young people skateboarding back and forth and there are tourists and there're all the street performers, acrobats, sword swallowers, clothing vendors, homeless people, and they're swarming about . . . the smog has curled up and wrapped itself around the edge of the water and all these people are choking and coughing . . . and several of them are pointing up in the air at me and the dragon, and I realize that the worlds of magic and reality are starting to converge . . . that, like the wizard told me, my talent for wizardry is overtaking my skill, and I'm starting to make the illusion too solid, starting to change the nature of reality itself. It's mostly kids who're pointing at the dragon. I guess many kids can still see a little ways into the worlds within. But if this goes on, and the dragon becomes completely real, then everyone will see it.

Yeah. The armor's getting heavy too. The illusion is slipping. And it's totally slipping in the wrong direction.

We're out over the beach now. My armor's getting heavy. My horse can barely sustain itself in the air . . . How can it? It's against the laws of physics for a horse with wings to be able to dart and hover and soar the way I've been doing.

Maybe I wounded the dragon back there in Griffith Park, but it doesn't seem to have slowed it down any. It's swooping down on me now. I'm tired. The horse is folding in on itself, morphing back into a skateboard. I can hear the whisper of the Pacific.

And here I am. Face-to-face with the dragon. My enchanted skateboard collapsing onto the concrete pathway with a thud. And the dragon huge now, gorged with a city's waste, opening his jaws wide and preparing to swallow. I think about running but before I can even turn, the dragon coils himself around me and I'm completely engulfed in the dragon. The dragon's flanks are fifty-foot walls, and when I look up, the sky is completely blocked by the dragon's face. There's no escape. I have to think fast.

I try the direct approach. I'm all, "Go away. I order you to go away."

The dragon just laughs.

Oh, God, I'm scared. I think of Dad, happily blowing up kangaroos in the studio, and Mom, buying up half the jewelry in Thailand, neither of them realizing for a moment that their son is about to flunk the test of destiny. Do they even care? I think bitterly. At least I won't have to tell their lawyers which one I'm going to pick to live with. I'll be gone, and the dragon can eat up the world.

Then I realize that *that's* my inner darkness. I'm mad because I feel they've walked out on me . . . I feel they've left me to fend for myself in the magic kingdom of Encino, thinking that if I *have* everything I won't notice that they're running out on me. I've been masquerading as, like, this cool, unflappable teenager, and inside me there's all this rage that's been eating away at me. And somehow I feel that *I'm* the cause of all this, that I'm the center of their storm, that it's all my fault.

Then I realize something else: The mirror, too, is a piece of my soul. And it shows things the way I see them. That's why I've been afraid to gaze into it for long. I'm scared I may see myself the way I really think of myself. And I've known for a long time that, in spite of all my pretenses, I see myself as kind of a nobody. I don't love myself at all. I feel small and useless and insignificant. Maybe because I was afraid of all the rage I kept coiled up inside me like a sleeping dragon.

I know what I have to do now.

And that's when I take the mirror out of my back pocket. Finally I know what it's for. At last I realize that this is all a big test—the kind of test that accounts for 100 percent of your grade—and now that I understand the question, there's only one answer that makes sense. Like most everything in fantasy, we're in an all-or-nothing situation. No test is a true test unless the universe is at stake. The world inside one person is as great as the whole cosmos, maybe greater, and the two are mirrors of each other, reflecting each other's truth, always and forever.

I don't look into the mirror. Instead, I turn it away from me, right toward the dragon's eyes.

Nothing happens for a moment.

And then, all at once, there's like this rumbling . . . the aluminum cans start to clatter and tinkle. A few drop off and clank on the concrete. And then the whole dragon starts to like dissolve. I mean, the skin comes peeling off, the eyes kind of melt, the teeth start chattering and then they break into a million pieces that flutter into the wind, and then, in a few quick breaths, the whole monstrosity dissipates into the ocean breeze . . . and the smog begins to lift . . and, as the last rays of the sun shine over the beach, stars start to come out.

They are like, the first stars we've seen over Los Angeles since the big smog alert of three months ago.

Then I see that Dad is walking down the footpath toward me. Penelope's beside him. When she sees that I'm still standing, she runs toward me, and she's all, "Aaron, thank God you're alive," and I'm about to say, "Well, like, how did you know I'd be here?" and Dad's all, "Congratulations, son!" and

I wonder what he means and how much he knows, and before I can say anything at all, there's a tap on my shoulder and I realize that Anaxagoras is here with us.

"Did he pass?" Dad asks him.

There's just a hint of a smile on Anaxagoras's lips. "Maybe," he says. And then he starts to laugh.

16

And Now: Lesson Two

"You did it!" Penelope was saying. "You passed! Your dad was telling me all about it! Oh, like, this is *so* exciting!"

"Wait a minute," I said. "Dad—did you know?"

Dad said, "Of course I did. You're a minor . . . I had to sign the release form before Anaxagoras could recruit you."

"But you never said anything!"

"Well," Dad said, "that's the big secret of all special effects, isn't it? Not telling. I didn't want to shatter the illusion. Anyhow, you seem to have gotten through lesson one in one piece . . . so I guess the new coach is a big success."

"Yeah," I said. "'But was all this just lesson one? The plumbing? The dragon? I mean, talk about throwing me into the deep end!"

And Anaxagoras said, rather sternly, "It was all part of the first lesson, Aaron. The plumbing, the Porsche, the pollution . . . you have to conquer yourself before you can conquer others . . . and magic is a sink-or-swim business."

"Yeah," said Dad. "*I* didn't make the grade, in the final analysis. I can't concentrate enough or something. I had to settle for the magic of motion pictures. But my son is getting the real thing."

The two of them winked at each other and I suddenly realized that they knew each other . . . probably had for *years*. In fact, didn't what Dad just tell me mean that he'd once tried out for sorcerer's apprentice too? I saw the wistful way Dad looked at me, and at the mirror that I was putting back into my pocket . . . and I realized that, for all that he was the greatest in his field, there were still things he yearned for . . . things he might never attain. He could still dream, and that's what kept the magic going in his life.

I didn't feel smug or superior because I'd passed the test and Dad hadn't. I mean, I didn't want *anyone* to have to go through what I'd just gone through. I still didn't know if I'd won by my talent or by sheer dumb luck. I had known from the moment I felt the presence of the darkness—that first day at Mrs. Leibowitz's—that one day I would have to fight it. I was certain that it wasn't totally over either; the war between the light and the dark goes on forever. That's why the universe is so precariously balanced, like our environment, and why it is so precious. Everything—*everything*—is joined in a cosmic chain, and no matter how insignificant you think you are, you're a link that cannot be broken.

I was all totally standing there gaping at all this cosmic truth, drinking in the wonder of it all, so I guess I must have looked pretty stupid. I kind of snapped to when I heard Penelope giggling a little.

I said to her, "How did you know to find me here?"

And she said, "Well, it was obvious, you doofus. The smog ends at the sea. I had to go find your dad because I needed a ride here. But when I got to your house he was already on his way. He knew something was afoot because he saw the freak smog attack on CNN."

"I saw what others didn't see when it was on the news," Dad said. "I saw that the smog was coiled up in the shape of a dragon." And from that I knew that Dad hadn't totally lost his talent for seeing the reality behind the illusion.

Slowly we walked away from the beach, toward the parking lot. Skaters whizzed up and down the footpath. Things were returning to normal. Everyone was looking at the stars. You don't see them too often around here, but tonight they were as clear and beautiful as though we were in the middle of the Mojave Desert. It's hard to believe there are so many of them. Thousands and thousands of them. Like, it makes you think.

Okay, so I was still the child of a dysfunctional family, and I was still going to go back to a house divided down the middle, and be Ping-Ponged back and forth, and have to deal with the divorce lawyers . . . but something *had* changed. I didn't hate myself anymore.

Sadly I said, "There's only one thing missing from all this . . . Mom's still in Bangkok, missing all the excitement." I thought Dad would get mad at my mentioning her, but he didn't even make any jokes about the cholesterol police.

"Well . . . ," Anaxagoras said, "it *is* around breakfast time there now . . . Perhaps we can all join her."

"And be back in time for school?" said Penelope.

"How in the world can we do that?" I said.

"You'd need a flying carpet or something!" Penelope said.

Anaxagoras stopped. His robes fluttered in the breeze, and little stars flashed out of his eyes. He patted me on the head, and said, "Well, Aaron, if you're not *too* tired after your test, perhaps we can go ahead and start you off on lesson two."

. . . and this is how I will leave Aaron Maguire, sorcerer's apprentice, taking his first steps on the long road to wisdom.

I, Anaxagoras the mage, have had many apprentices, on this world and on many others, and it is always the first days that are the most difficult.

Perhaps it will come as no surprise that the house split down the middle became a happier house, and in time the dividing line became blurred. Aaron's happiness was an infectious thing, and it softened his parents' loneliness, and it dulled their bitterness; and because they saw that the goodness in him was a mirror of the goodness in both of them, they no longer saw each other as enemies . . . not, I must add, that they ever came to love each other as they had before, and not that their marriage was rescued—for total reconciliation is the stuff of fairy tales—but they were no longer angry.

Yes, in the city of Los Angeles, on the northern slopes of the Santa Monica Mountains, there lies a magic kingdom called Encino. It is not magic because of the glittering shopping malls, the Japanese bank buildings, sushi bars, and German cars; it is not the video arcades, fast-food havens, and casually dressed people with wallets full of credit cards, nor the neon, the palm trees, or the smog. These things are marvelous, but they are not magic.

As always, the one true magic springs from the human heart.